A Lesson IN Love

HARPER BLISS

OTHER HARPER BLISS BOOKS
Life in Bits (with T.B. Markinson)
A Swing at Love (with Caroline Bliss)
No Greater Love than Mine
Once Upon a Princess (with Clare Lydon)
In the Distance There Is Light
The Road to You
Seasons of Love
Release the Stars
Once in a Lifetime
At the Water's Edge
The French Kissing Series
High Rise (The Complete Collection)

THE PINK BEAN SERIES
More Than Words
Crazy for You
Love Without Limits
No Other Love
Water Under Bridges
This Foreign Affair
Everything Between Us
Beneath the Surface
No Strings Attached

Copyright © 2019 by Harper Bliss
Cover pictures © Depositphotos / swisshippo / seqoya / panco
Cover design by Caroline Manchoulas
Published by Ladylit Publishing – a division of Q.P.S. Projects Limited -
Hong Kong
ISBN-13 978-988-79124-4-6

1

HELEN

I have ten minutes before my next appointment and I instinctively reach for my phone. My finger hovers over my trusty dictation app, but I catch myself. *Not here.*

With a sigh, I put my phone back. When I arrived this morning, I was in the middle of dictating a climactic scene. But it would have seemed too odd to sit talking to myself in my car in the car park so I stopped—although, these days, so many of us look like we're talking to ourselves all the time.

These are my university hours and I can't allow my two schedules to get confused, even though my office door is closed and no one would see me.

Instead, I grab the sheet of paper I printed out earlier from my desk. Victoria Carlisle. Sounds posh. But I've taught myself not to judge—if that's even possible. This is Oxford. There's no shortage of posh people here. I've seen many students come and go over the years, from all backgrounds, but the majority have always been more posh than not.

I glance at Victoria Carlisle's picture. The department makes it compulsory to have your picture on its website. Could she be the very last student I supervise?

"You very well might be, Victoria Carlisle," I say to her printed image. Dark hair. Brown eyes. Wide, full lips. She must have been in one of my first-year lectures, but if she was, I don't remember—despite her distinctive mouth.

Someone knocks on the door.

"Yes." I drop the sheet of paper.

The door opens and in walks the woman whose picture I was just studying.

"Hello, Professor Swift." She walks straight towards me, hand outstretched. "I'm Victoria."

I briefly take her hand in mine, then invite her to sit.

She's wearing jeans and a turtleneck sweater. Her hair is pulled into a ponytail.

"Right," she says and looks me straight in the eye, flashing a very wide smile. "I have to admit"—her voice is clear—"I'm a little nervous."

Her attitude and facial expression contradict her statement. Since her arrival, the energy in my office has shifted. She's one of those people who draw the eye—who light up a room. I wouldn't be caught dead using that cliché in one of my novels.

"No need for that." She's making *me* nervous now. One day, if she does get her doctorate, she'll make an outstanding lecturer—unlike me, perhaps. With some people, one glance is all it takes to know they'll excel.

"The way I see it"—she cocks her head—"you're my only chance at doing this particular kind of in-depth research."

I arch up my eyebrows. I know what Victoria Carlisle wants to research. She emailed me about it in astonishing detail.

"I wouldn't put it in such black and white terms, Miss Carlisle."

"Well, no doubt you know what I mean." That wide grin again, accompanied by a wink this time. Goodness, this woman is forward. Like most young people these days, who carry themselves with a familiarity towards faculty that I've never quite got used to.

Of course I know what she means. "Professor Monohan has an interest in the subject you suggest."

Victoria shakes her head. "She doesn't really."

"Did you inquire with her?"

"I did and she wouldn't even meet with me to discuss it."

That figures. "So I'm your second choice?"

"Most definitely not, Professor," she's quick to say. "You were always my first choice, but I felt like I needed to hedge my bets."

"You didn't try Professor Fleming?" I ask, more to amuse myself than anything else.

She cocks her head again. "No, of course not." Now she's making me sound silly for even suggesting it.

"All right." It's time to move things along. "So, the evolution of lesbian characters in English literature in the twentieth and twenty-first centuries."

Victoria nods.

"I take it you have considered this subject carefully?" Another silly question, but one I find myself asking every time nonetheless.

"My master's thesis was about lesbian pulp fiction of the fifties and sixties, so a doctoral dissertation would really be an expansion of that. I feel like there's much more to be said on the subject and a DPhil dissertation carries more weight."

"You seem very passionate about the subject." I take my time to examine her face more carefully this time.

"I am, indeed." She sits up a little straighter. "In almost every aspect of life, lesbians are the most invisible group. Regardless of the reasons for that, it's my mission to unearth as many lesbian characters as I can in the last hundred years of English literature. It *is* very much my passion."

"Good." I give her an encouraging nod. The goal of this first meeting is always to gauge and predict—insofar as that's possible—the stamina of the DPhil candidates. The dropout rate is so high, and so many promising dissertations never get finished. I, for one, would like to read the final version of this particular project. At the moment, Victoria Carlisle surely comes across as very enthusiastic. I see a determination in her glance I rarely encounter. This could be one that works out. "I'd be very happy to be your supervisor."

"Yes!" Victoria bumps her fist into the air.

I can't help but smile a little. It bolsters my enthusiasm for my own job just a bit. The fondness for it that I seem to have lost along the way. It's been a while since someone like Victoria has come along. One more year full-time, I tell myself. By the end of this year, my other supervisees will have completed their dissertations and working part-time will give me more than enough hours to supervise Victoria. To help this woman get started with her research. I can actually see myself do it now.

Victoria regroups and puts her hands in her lap.

"The first few months, I'll see you once a week." I'm already looking forward to discussing Victoria's quest for lesbian characters in literature. When I was a student, it wouldn't have been entirely unthinkable to devote a dissertation to this type of subject, but it would have taken a lot more convincing to get the whole thing off the ground. I also didn't have any out-and-proud professors to turn to. Today, in the Faculty of English Language and Literature alone, there are three of us—with a lot of suspicion surrounding a fourth.

"I look forward to it, Professor Swift," Victoria says.

2

RORY

Professor Swift has no idea how much I look forward to working with her. I had kind of hoped she'd want to see me twice a week to discuss my progress—or take me out to lunch to celebrate. But I'll take once a week. I'll take whatever I can get.

I glance at her, wondering if she'll have anything else to say or ask. Maybe she'll want to inquire about my research methods or perhaps she'd like a copy of my master's thesis. I have one just for her in my bag.

She moves her mouse and looks at her screen.

"Shall we say Mondays at three?"

"Okay." I don't even consult my calendar. I'll make time regardless.

"Was there anything else?" Professor Swift's light blue gaze goes a little steely all of a sudden.

"Um, no." I came to this meeting prepared. I have all the answers to her possible questions at the ready in my head, but she doesn't appear to have any. Perhaps she had already decided to take me on before seeing me. She doesn't appear to be the most talkative type. There's a lot of inquisition in that icy gaze of hers, however.

"I take it you know what to do next?" There's a hint of doubt in her voice.

"I do." Resolutely, I jump out of my seat. "I'll report back next week." I offer my hand.

She eyes it for a split second, then stands and takes it in hers. She gives me a curt nod before releasing my hand.

I exit Professor Swift's office and once I've closed the door behind me, bump my fist into the air again.

When I decided to go for my DPhil I only ever wanted to do it on this subject and with Professor Swift as my supervisor. I might have gone to Professor Fleming if Swift had refused to supervise me, but it wouldn't have been the same, what with Fleming being a man.

I walk out of the building's stuffy hallway feeling like I've won the lottery. In a way, I have. This should also keep Mother and Father happy with me for a few more years.

"Swift's on board," I shout as soon as I walk into our apartment. I don't even know if Jessica's home.

She leaps from the kitchen into the lounge. "You wooed the ice maiden." She puts her hands on her hips. "Go you."

I chuckle. "I hardly wooed her."

"You know what Sarah told me." Jess walks to the drinks cabinet. "G&T to celebrate?"

"Is that what Sarah told you?" I beam a smile over to her.

She rolls her eyes at me. "You want one or not?"

"Do you even have to ask?" Jess and I are both DPhil students, both of us lingering in limbo between student and 'real' life. We can have a gin and tonic before lunch any day of the week.

"On it, darling," Jess says.

"What *did* Professor Monohan tell you?"

She turns around to roll her eyes at me again. "I take it Swift will never let you call her by her first name, but *Sarah* and I are very much on a first-name basis. Have been from day one."

"Yes, yes, I know. You've told me often." I let myself fall onto the sofa.

"Sarah told me she'd be very surprised if Swift took on any new DPhil students to supervise this year." Jess arches her eyebrows.

"I must have some really serious powers of persuasion then." I wink at her.

She turns towards the drinks cabinet again. I hear the sizzle of a can of tonic being opened.

"You really must, Rory," Jess says with her back to me. "I should know, after all."

I ignore Jess's comment and think about the brief amount of time I spent in Professor Swift's office. I didn't have to persuade her at all. Professor Sarah Monohan must have assumed wrongly.

"There you go, darling." Jess hands me a glass filled to the absolute brim. "Cheers." When she clinks hers against mine, some liquid sloshes over the top. Sometimes, I feel like we still live a bit too much like students.

"Now that it's official," she says, "you should come to lunch with Sarah and Alistair tomorrow. We'll have a gay old time." She grins at me.

"Christ, Jess." I take a large sip and inwardly admonish myself for not picking a more subtle kind of person as a roommate.

"Sarah's much more forthcoming than Swift *and* she's rather fond of a boozy lunch. Think of all the background information you can get out of her."

"I'll see." I glance at my friend. We've been living together for three years and I know what she's like—a loud busy-body who likes to throw a party every other week.

"Fuck that, Rory. You're coming," Jessica says. "I know you better than you know yourself. You want to come."

"Don't you have a Tinder date to get all dolled up for?"

"Not today," Jess says on a sigh. "In fact, not this week or this month or this year."

"Has the well of eligible Oxford bachelors run dry?"

She expels another sigh. "I should have stuck with you, Rory." She paints on another grin. "We had a good time together."

"For about a week or two, maybe." We've had this conversation so many times before, usually over a couple of drinks.

"I could have been married to Victoria Carlisle by now," Jess muses. "Acquired myself a piece of your family's fortune along the way."

"I hate to break it to you—again," I catch her gaze. "But it's hardly a fortune and, besides, my mother would not have welcomed you into the family with open arms. She's not really a very open-armed kind of person."

"What are you talking about? Lady Carlisle adores me." Jessica bats her lashes.

"Sure, as long as you're nothing more than my friend."

Jessica shrugs and takes a large gulp of gin and tonic. Even she doesn't have a comeback for that one.

3

HELEN

As always, when I walk to my car—my midlife-crisis-on-wheels, as Alistair likes to call it—I try to get back into the story I'm in the middle of writing. I like to start dictating as soon as I drive out of the car park. My protagonist, Detective Orla Parish, is about to stumble upon another important clue.

"Helen," I hear a voice behind me. I recognise it all too well.

I turn around. "Sarah." I flash her a smile.

"Care for a drink in The Maiden's Head?"

I try to sigh quietly. I point at my car—I was so close to it. If only I had left my office a minute earlier, I would have been driving away right now, getting ready to dictate. "I'm driving."

"Don't you usually stay in Oxford on Wednesdays?" She cocks her head.

"I'm, um, working on something at home. Hence all the back and forth."

"Must be quite something." It's more a question than a statement, but I'm not going to tell Sarah what my project is. She'd only sneer at it—and I wouldn't even be able to fault her for her reaction. "Come on. One glass of vino isn't going to stop you from driving home, is it?"

It will most certainly stop me from adding a few much-needed pages to my manuscript, and I'm already behind. I also have an inbox full of emails waiting to be replied to.

"Sure." My problem, for the longest time, was that I could never say no to Sarah. "One drink."

"Come on then." She hooks her arm through mine—something she would never have done on campus while we were still together—and we head to the pub.

"You didn't run into me by sheer coincidence," Sarah says as soon as we've sat down with a glass of red wine in front of us. "I need to tell you something."

"Sounds ominous." I stare into her face. Her long brown hair is gorgeously curly. Her eyes are dark and broody.

"I just wanted you to hear it from me first. I've... started seeing someone."

For a split second, it feels as though the gulp of wine I've just swallowed might make its way back up. Breaking up with Sarah was one of the hardest things I've ever had to do in my life.

"Who's the lucky lady?" I manage to ask. I take a deep breath and regroup. It was bound to happen at some point, of course.

"She's not in academia," Sarah says, as though that's a huge achievement. "In fact, she has nothing to do with the university whatsoever."

I just nod. I know that what she really means to say is: as opposed to you.

"You're not going to believe what she does for a living, Helen." There's a glow in Sarah's eyes that I find hard to stomach.

"Really?"

"She's a plumber." Sarah sounds almost triumphant.

"Oh. Well, I suppose I can guess how you met then."

Sarah shakes her head. "I didn't hire her to fix my pipes." She holds my gaze. "I met her at this *thing* for lesbians."

Now I really do a double-take. "What 'thing' for lesbians?"

"A gathering, I guess."

"You went to a lesbian 'gathering'?" I make no effort to hide the incredulity in my voice.

"After we broke up... well, it took me a while to see that perhaps you, um, were right about some things."

"Good for you." I take another deep breath. Sarah is someone I cared for deeply—someone I loved—so I have no other choice but be happy for her. She can barely keep from bursting into a grin when mentioning the plumber. "What's her name?"

"Joan." She lets the grin fully come through now. "Joan Arnott."

"I'm happy for you." I twirl my glass between my fingers, hesitating between gulping it fast and leaving it as it is and getting out of here. I need some time to process that my ex, who couldn't overcome her discomfort with being seen out and about with a woman—especially a fellow professor—is now seeing a plumber she met at a lesbian gathering.

"I've been so nervous about telling you." Most of the tension has drained from Sarah's voice.

"We broke up more than three years ago. There was really no need to be nervous at all."

Sarah slants her head. "There was a little."

I give her a curt nod.

"I long for the day you tell me you've met a plumber." She gives me a dazzling smile. "But I'm not sure there are *that* many lesbian plumbers in Oxfordshire. Perhaps a carpenter." She sits a little straighter. "Maybe, next time, you should join Joan and me when we go to the... lesbian gathering."

"I'm not going somewhere to meet women with my ex and her new lover." I purse my lips. "Besides, I'm not looking. I'm perfectly happy with my life." That's not entirely true, of course. The truth is that I have no idea where in my life I'd fit in a special someone, between my full-time job at the university and my hobby that has got way out of hand.

"Is that why you bought that Porsche? Because you're so happy?"

"As a matter of fact, it is."

Sarah eyes me quizzically, but I'm not about to explain things to her in more detail.

"It doesn't look like it." She leans over the table. "In fact, you look a little tired, Helen. Are you getting enough sleep?"

"Probably not, but I plough on."

She squints at me, then says. "Jess told me you're thinking about taking on another DPhil student."

"Jess?"

"Jessica Malone, who I'm supervising."

I shake my head at Sarah's over-familiarity with the students she supervises. I've seen her and said Jessica having lunch together many a time—something I would never consider doing with the people I have a supervisory relationship with. "That's right. I've agreed to take her on."

"Couldn't resist her?"

"What?"

"Last time we spoke, you said you'd had your fill of DPhil's. Mind you, you'd had a bit too much wine." Sarah winks at me.

"She might very well be the last one," I say wistfully.

Sarah raises her glass. "You're only forty-nine, Helen. I fear the university might disagree, but let's drink to that, anyway."

We clink rims and I know that Sarah is drinking to her plumber rather than my resolution to cut back my hours at the university. As long as I don't tell her about my other career, she has no way of knowing my real motives.

✣ 4 ✣

RORY

J essica was right, Professor Monohan sure does favour a boozy lunch. She's one of those people who can't bear the sight of a half-empty glass. She keeps topping up my wine as soon as I've taken a sip.

We're occupying a large table outside The Maiden's Head. Apart from Jessica and me, there are two other DPhil candidates at lunch, along with Professor Fleming.

I'm seated next to Professor Fleming, who insists that I call him Alistair.

"I'm surprised that Helen agreed to supervise you, but now that I know the subject of your dissertation, I can see why she wouldn't have been able to resist." He speaks in a low voice so only I can hear him. As usual, Jess is making enough noise to drown out any other voices. "It's right up her alley."

"It's right up mine as well, so it should be a good fit."

"Helen can be very motivational if she wants to be, so I don't think you'll be disappointed."

"Even though everyone keeps saying that she's clearly sick of supervising students." I look into Alistair's sparkly eyes. He has the gaze of an adolescent: bright-eyed and always wandering.

"Here's a secret for you," he whispers. "Every single person on this earth gets sick of their job sometimes, no matter how much they enjoy it. That's life." He goes silent for a few seconds. "Although I can't shake the impression that with Helen, there's something else going on. I just can't figure out what it is. At first, I thought she had a new, very secret lover. Someone she consistently has to rush home to Chewford for, but—"

"Professor Swift lives in Chewford?"

"Upper Chewford. Yes," Alistair confirms. "Why?"

"I'm from around there. My parents live on the outskirts of Upper Chewford." If there is even such a thing as the outskirts of Upper Chewford. The village is about the size of a postage stamp.

"A country girl." He squints at me. "I can see it now. You look... very wholesome in that countryside way."

"I haven't lived in Chewford for a long time."

"Tell me about your academic trajectory, Rory." He leans back and eyes me eagerly. I conclude there and then that I like Professor Alistair Fleming very much.

I tell him all about doing my undergrad and obtaining my first master's degree at Cambridge, after which I came down to Oxford to do another master's degree, and finally ended up going for a DPhil.

"Ah, the quintessential eternal student." He nods as though he has seen many of my kind throughout his career. "You might end up being one of us at some point. Between you and me, it's not too bad a life." He grins mischievously.

"Apart from all those pesky students you have to deal with," I say, grinning back.

"I love my DPhil students. The majority of them are much more mature than the undergrads I lecture to." He rolls his eyes. "Mind you, they all think they're *very* mature—it comes with the age—while they're all still so wet behind the ears. It's quite endearing, actually." The corners of his mouth quirk upward. "Ah, I'm just lucky. I love what I do. Look at me sitting here, getting acquainted with a bright young lass from Upper Chewford."

"You might be selling a false image of your job to me. I take it that having leisurely lunches is not what you do most of?"

"Indeed, I am *not* a lady who lunches." He winks at me. "There is some transference of knowledge, of course. And quite a bit of time spent in stuffy classrooms. And faculty meetings and the like. The paperwork keeps increasing every term as well, or so it seems, even though I believed we were meant to live in a paperless age now."

"Alistair," Professor Monohan says. "Stop quizzing Rory."

"I'm doing no such thing."

"He was just telling me the pros and cons of being a lecturer," I say.

Monohan and Alistair strike up a conversation, which I don't follow in detail, because I'm still processing that Professor Swift lives in Upper Chewford. She may very well know my family, or at least know *of* them.

I'm not sure how I feel about that yet.

After lunch, I'm supposed to go back to campus and work on my research plan, but I've had a bit too much wine. I decide to head home for a quick nap—sans Jess, who is so used to boozy lunches with her supervisor, she can go straight back to work after.

I walk along the manicured lawns that, somehow, seem much greener than the ones in my parents' gardens. I was surprised that, last time she came to visit, my mother didn't comment on that.

It's the beginning of autumn and some of the leaves are starting to turn. I revel in the thought that I'll be staying at Oxford a few more years. I feel so at home here. Jess should finish her DPhil this year, if she cuts back on the boozy lunches. I hope she stays in Oxford. I'd hate to lose my roommate.

I'm still lost in my thoughts, even though they're a bit of a swimming mess, when I clock a familiar figure coming towards me. I straighten my spine and hope my face isn't too flushed from the wine.

Now that we're in an official relationship, should I stop and greet her formally? Or just nod? I don't even know why I'm second-guessing myself like this. If it were anyone else, I'd stop to have a quick chat. But Professor Swift doesn't register in my mind as just anyone.

I raise my hand and give an awkward little wave.

"Taken up questionable habits already, have we?" Professor Swift takes me completely by surprise. "I spotted Professors Fleming and Monohan with their posse at The Maiden's Head."

"My roommate, Jessica, is working with Professor Monohan. She coerced me into joining them." Why do I feel the need to come up with an excuse, anyway?

"You do what you want with your time, Miss Carlisle."

Everyone calls me Rory, I want to say—buoyed by the wine, no doubt—but I manage to hold my tongue.

"I will have the beginnings of an outline and my research plan ready for you on Monday." I stand to attention a little bit more. Professor Swift is taller than me and I feel myself wither a little under her gaze.

"I look forward to it." She makes to continue on her path, but I feel like prolonging our impromptu conversation. I don't think I'll have many chances to chat to Professor Swift while I'm slightly inebriated.

"Alist—I mean Professor Fleming told me you live in Upper Chewford."

She gives me a curt nod.

"I grew up in Chewford. I've been away a while, but it's so gorgeous and peaceful there, I always enjoy going back." This is not entirely true. Whereas the village is gorgeous, many of the villagers—and most of my immediate family—don't know how to deal with me.

"What a coincidence." She tilts her head. "Are you one of *those* Carlisles, perhaps?"

"Depends what you mean by 'those'." As ever, when my family is mentioned, I'm never sure whether to feel amused or annoyed.

"The Chewford Carlisles, who live on the estate on the edge of the village."

"The youngest and most disappointing of their progeny," I half-joke. Oops. The wine might be getting the better of me.

Professor Swift ignores my remark—just like my parents would.

"Interesting," she says. "I really must go now." She glances at her watch. "See you Monday." With that, she saunters off, leaving me a little flustered in her wake.

✿ 5 ✿

HELEN

On Saturday morning, I get up early as usual. I need to revise the chapters I managed to dictate the day before. I need to reply to a few dozen emails. I need to look into finding a virtual assistant who can make my life a little less busy. I also need to go over edits for my next book.

I've just got out of bed and I'm already tired just thinking about the sheer volume of things to do on what's supposed to be a day off.

When I started writing fiction, it was just a bit of fun. A wonderful way to while away some free time—which, after Sarah and I broke up, I found myself having too much of. Now, the whole business seems to have taken on a life of its own. Not a day goes by that I don't get an email asking when my next book will be out. I certainly never would have guessed that my cozy Cotswolds mysteries would spark such interest, although cozies have been a guilty pleasure of mine since I learned how to read. It seems I'm not alone in that.

But I really shouldn't complain about it. If only I could talk to someone. A real live person who understands what's it like to juggle two full-time jobs, of which one was never meant to be more than a hobby. A hobby I can't get enough of. When I'm lecturing, I often find myself thinking about Orla Parish—the main character in all my books—and the current crime she's trying to solve. It's stronger than myself. It's a distraction, really. This endless tug of war between wanting to do my university job well and indulging my creative side.

Just like Sarah confessed to me that she's fallen head-over-heels for a plumber, perhaps I can confess to her that I write cozy mysteries. If I can confess to Sarah, I can tell anyone. After all, she's the one who relentlessly mocked my book collection when she first browsed my shelves.

"For an English Lit professor, you have a surprisingly low-brow taste in fiction," were her exact words.

"One does not exclude the other," I rebuffed her comment, but she just shrugged disdainfully.

On leisurely Sunday mornings, while she was studying *The Telegraph* from cover to cover, she'd often ask if I was reading one of my fluffy novels again. At least I don't go drinking with my students, I used to think. I still think so now. We both had our quirks, I guess, and in the end, it wasn't those differences that drove us apart.

These days, I can only dream of a leisurely Sunday morning. But at least today is Saturday. If I can cross all the items off my to-do list today, I will reward myself with a visit to the pub down the road tonight. I need to speak to Josie and inform her that I can't do the monthly quiz night any longer. Something will have to give—and that's the only thing I can let go of right now.

I stumble into the shower and wait until the water's nice and hot. It takes a while before my shoulders relax, even under the soothing warm water. I'm too stressed for my own good. Maybe more will have to give than quiz night at The Golden Fleece.

~

When I arrive at The Golden Fleece, my usual table in the nook next to the bookcase isn't free. Josie gives me an apologetic smile. The past few years, the Cotswolds tourist season seems to have become never-ending. A loud American family occupies my second favourite table. I decide to sit at the bar.

"Swamped again." I smile at Josie.

"You won't hear me complain. How are you, Helen?"

I don't want to say 'busy'. 'Fine' used to be the most common answer to that age-old question. Now, it has become 'busy, busy, busy'. "I'm very well. And you?"

"Busy," Josie says.

I can't help but chuckle. But Josie *is* actually very busy. She's not working in the pub alone, thank goodness.

"What can I get you? The usual?"

I nod. I've been looking forward to this gin and tonic all day long.

When she puts it in front of me, I ask, "Can I talk to you about something when you have a minute?"

"Sure." She fixes her gaze on me. "What's up?"

"It really pains me to have to do this, but as of next month, I won't be able to run the quiz night any longer. I'll do this month's, of course. I'm so sorry."

"Oh, Helen. Really? You've been running the quiz night forever. Did you get yourself a new girlfriend? Because that's the only excuse Mum will accept, you know." She grins at me as if it's a foregone conclusion that I've met someone new.

I shake my head. "I've been... freelancing on the side and it has all become a bit much." Why can't I just come out and tell her I've been writing in my spare time? Why is it so difficult? I swear, this is harder than coming out as a lesbian.

"Freelancing? Doing what? MC'ing quizzes around the Cotswolds?" Josie doesn't lose her smile.

"Consulting work. All very boring," I quickly reply.

"You're going to have to tell Mum yourself, Helen. She thinks your quizzes are far superior to any other in the greater Oxfordshire area, what with you being such a distinguished Oxford professor and all that."

"I'll stop by tomorrow to tell her." I sip from my gin and tonic.

"I'll try to soften the blow a little beforehand." Josie shoots me a wink, before rushing off to help another customer. I turn around on my barstool and see that my preferred table has freed up. I decide to linger at the bar a bit longer, just to chat to Josie while I enjoy my gin and tonic.

For the first time all week I start to relax.

✿ 6 ✿

RORY

A s I drive through Upper Chewford, I can't help but think about Professor Swift. What does she do on Sundays? Go to her local pub for a roast, perhaps? Whatever she's doing right now, it can only be a million times more exciting than the family gathering I'm about to attend. There are only a few of these occasions I can't get out of. My perfect brother's birthday lunch is one of them.

I reach the gate and, almost immediately, it opens. I do still come home often enough for George to recognise my car and throw the gates wide for me. Or maybe Daddy has installed a new alarm system again, a state-of-the-art one that recognises number plates. The truth is that I have no clue what my father's been up to lately, although he's the member of my family I get along with best.

You'd think it would be my brother, because we're closer in age, but ever since he married Brenda, it's as though he's turning more and more into our mother. It has been a bewitching, and rather scary, process to witness.

By the time I've parked, the front door is open. George, who's been working for my family since before I was born, is the only one to come out to greet me. My brother's car is already there so I conclude my parents are too busy fawning over their grandchildren—also perfect specimens of humanity, even though all they do at this age is make a hell of a lot of noise—to notice their youngest daughter's arrival.

"Miss Rory," George says. "How wonderful to see you."

"And you." I refrain from giving George a playful pat on the arm, knowing very well that it would make him uncomfortable. "How are you, George?"

"I'm very well, Miss Rory. And yourself?"

"Can't complain, although I'm sure I'll feel a lot better on my way out." I wink at him.

"You mustn't say things like that, my dear. You know the walls have ears in this place."

"Has mother had the entrance hall bugged?" I smile at him. I wouldn't put it past her.

George just shakes his head.

I take a deep breath and head to the drawing room, ready to confront my family.

"Victoria," my mother says, and throws her arms wide. As though she's genuinely happy to see me. She might be today. Who knows? After all, I came alone. I didn't request explicit permission to bring a 'friend', as my mother has always called my girlfriends. I once made the mistake of bringing someone unannounced, after which the 'explicit permission' rule was promptly born.

My brother, of course, has always been allowed to bring home anyone he pleased, as long as they were of the opposite sex—and of a certain *pedigree*.

"Good to see you, darling," Mother says, and holds me in

her arms for a split second. Prolonged hugs have always been considered a display of weakness in my family.

My father doesn't even hug me. He just gives my shoulder a quick squeeze.

"Happy birthday, Tommy." I can barely kiss my brother on the cheek because of the infant in his arms. "Where's Brenda?"

"She went outside with Emma. They both needed some air."

"Did the two of you come by yourselves?" I ask, hinting at the absence of the children's nanny.

"Abby's unwell. The flu." He rolls his eyes as though nannies are supposed to be above getting the flu. "We want to keep her away from the children while she's ill, obviously."

"Obviously." I wisely refrain from rolling my eyes.

"Here you go, Miss Rory." George has entered the room and hands me a glass of champagne.

"I could do with a top-up," my brother says. "Brenda's driving," he says in response to Mother's disapproving glare.

Mother doesn't seem to approve of that either, though. She probably thinks a man should drive his family home at all times.

He turns to me and shoots me an uncharacteristic wink. He seems to be in good spirits today. Matthew, my nephew, starts clawing at the champagne flute Tommy's holding.

"I'll take him, darling," Mother says.

Matthew doesn't seem too eager to be held by his granny. He starts wailing as soon as he has changed arms. Tommy gets rid of his drink, grabs the child, and takes him outside as well, leaving me alone with my parents.

"How are things at Oxford?" Daddy asks.

Mother guides us to the cluster of armchairs by the window and we sit.

"Very good. I got the supervisor I wanted."

Daddy doesn't inquire further about the subject of my dissertation, knowing full well it would make Mother unhappy to discuss it over pre-lunch drinks. The L word is not to be mentioned too often in this house. Although I can't have used up my monthly quota yet. I haven't seen my parents in a while.

"How's the flat?" Mum asks.

"Um, fine, I guess."

"I do hope you and what's-her-name don't throw too many parties. Having students live in a property devalues it terribly," she says, as though she needs the money.

"Her name's Jessica and we're hardly—" Before I get the chance to respond, my brother and his family make a loud entrance into the drawing room.

"Rory," Brenda shrieks, as though I'm one of her oldest friends. "It's been far too long."

I get up to greet her. Her hug is the warmest I've received today.

With their return, the peace and quiet is well and truly over, and all the attention is diverted back to Matthew, who's one, and Emma, who's four. We spend my brother's birthday lunch discussing the many astonishing feats of toddlers.

"It's amazing how quickly they learn, especially Matty, who just follows his big sister's lead," Brenda says more than once.

As much as I adore my niece and nephew, a few hours in their eardrum-assaulting company has me running for the hills as soon as I'm excused from the table. However, instead of escaping into the hills, I decide to walk into the village.

❦ 7 ❦

HELEN

I've just told Eugenie that I will have to relinquish my duties as monthly quizmaster—she took it better than expected.

The weather's mild so I take my half pint of Cotswolds IPA outside. Having a drink at my local on a Sunday afternoon is the only thing that seems to thoroughly relax me after a busy week and an equally busy weekend. It's four in the afternoon and I'm not doing anything else today, even though I should get started on the questions for the next—and my last—quiz. I've been in charge of The Golden Fleece quiz for so long, that surely I can recycle some older questions. I'll just throw in some new ones about the constant musical chairs game of new and resigning cabinet ministers, and I'll be good to go.

I sigh before I take a sip from my beer. If only I could 'wing it', as some of my students say. If only I had that kind of personality. But I'm not someone who 'wings' anything at all. Not even the slightest thing. Two decades of working with young people haven't taught me otherwise, so it's safe to assume I'll always be this uptight.

"Hi, Helen," Marc, my neighbour, says. "Mind if I join you?"

"Not at all." I gesture at the free chair next to me.

"Stacey and I were just talking about you. You haven't been to dinner at ours in months. Are you free this coming week?"

I'm never free, I think, but I recognise that's a little dramatic. I'd better save the drama for the stories I make up. "I would really love that, Marc."

"If this Indian summer persists, we could do a barbecue."

"That would be lovely." I drink my beer with a little more gusto, because sitting here chatting with my neighbour, and having just been invited to a relaxed meal, reminds me of how my life used to be. Of how it could be again. Over the summer, I contemplated cutting back my hours at the university to part-time, but it was too soon and too risky. I wasn't ready yet for that leap.

I bought a Porsche instead, which, in hindsight, was a little foolish. I should have saved the money and prepared better for what will be an inevitable decision.

"When you come over to ours," Marc says, a naughty note in his voice, "would you mind if we invite another friend?" He sits there grinning at me.

"Who did you have in mind?" I play along. It's not the first time my friendly neighbours have tried to set me up with another woman. As long as I'm single, I imagine it won't be the last.

"A new member of Stacey's choir. She sings contralto, apparently." For some reason, this statement is accompanied by a wink. "As soon as Stace met her, she said we should introduce her to you."

Bless their hearts, Marc and Stacey truly believe that all lesbians in the area will get along. That we have no choice because there are so few of us. Although they should know by now that the Cotswolds is very popular with all kinds of lesbians, not just the outdoorsy ones.

"What's her name?" I might as well ask. I'll be meeting this contralto soon enough.

"Mireille. She's as French as her name sounds."

I haven't dated anyone in such a long time that the mere fact she's French is enough to intrigue me.

"But she's lived in the UK for years," Marc says.

"Has Stacey told her all about me already?"

Marc nods enthusiastically. "Who wouldn't want to meet a woman like you, Helen? Mireille's very excited."

I suppress a groan. I'm not sure where Marc gets the idea that I'm such an eligible bachelorette. I'm just an overworked professor. I bet Stacey dropped *Oxford* a few times in the conversation she had about me. It can be enough to get some people terribly excited—for all the wrong reasons, I have learned throughout my career at the university.

Either way, I have nothing to lose. And I don't mind indulging my neighbours.

"I'd best get home to the Missus," Marc says. "I promised I'd only be out for one." He points at his empty pint.

"Are you sure I can't get you another?" I ask.

"Nah, I'm good. See you soon." He nods at me and saunters down the street. I follow him with my gaze. I can see my own house from here, but it hardly beckons me. No one is waiting for me. I allow myself to get a tad excited about meeting Mireille. You just never know.

As I continue to stare down the street, someone else pops up in my field of vision. Someone who sparks instant recognition, which is no surprise because I know everyone who lives on this street, even the couple that just moved in last month. It's impossible not to know your neighbours in Upper Chewford, even with the constant influx of burnt-out Londoners desperate for a quieter lifestyle.

I squint as the figure comes closer. She's not one of my neighbours. She's too young. Maybe one of their children home for the weekend? Dark hair. That distinct, full-lipped mouth.

It's Victoria Carlisle.

She did tell me that her family lives here. And now she just turns up in my local.

"Professor Swift." She paints on a broad smile.

"Miss Carlisle. Fancy seeing you here."

"I had a family lunch I desperately needed to get away from." She looks at the facade of The Golden Fleece. "Can you believe I've never set foot in this pub?"

"I'll take your word for it."

"I'm absolutely parched. Can I get you another?" She looks at my empty glass. "What are you having?"

I can't possibly drink with a student on a Sunday afternoon. But then I think of my empty house. And it's such a lovely day out.

"I'll have a Cotswolds IPA," I blurt out. It must be the one I've had already. If I keep this up, I'll be having lunch with Sarah and her DPhil students at the Maiden's Head soon.

"Coming right up." Victoria heads inside.

This gives me a minute to consider what I'm doing. I was just thinking about how uptight I can be. Maybe having a beer with my new student will absolve me of that, at least for today.

Live a little, Helen, I tell myself. You work hard enough.

❧ 8 ☙

RORY

The walk into the village was much longer than I remembered it. Before I place my order, I go into the ladies room to wash my hands and splash some water on my face.

While I wait for the drinks, I glance around the pub. **It's the epitome of the English country pub, complete with fireplace and an elderly gentleman snoozing behind a half-drunk pint in the adjacent nook.**

I may have grown up on the outskirts of Upper Chewford, but I clearly haven't seen much of the village. Years at boarding school, followed by almost a decade of university has made me forget all about it.

The walk into the village was so bloody gorgeous, it almost —almost—made me vow to come home more often. I'd have to find times when my parents are away, though. But the thought of spending a weekend at the family home with George pampering me sounds pretty good right now. Maybe next time Jess plans a party I really don't feel like attending.

The woman behind the bar makes my gaydar ping slightly, so I treat her to a lingering smile. You just never know. And how that would wind Mother up. Bringing home the local barmaid.

Chuckling to myself, I make my way outside.

"Here you go." I hold up my glass, ready to clink rims with Professor Swift.

"Thank you." She must consider it impolite to not toast with me and touches her glass against mine.

"It's quite a walk," I say. "I had underestimated it." How on earth am I going to get home? Does Upper Chewford have Uber? I'm not walking back. I can always call George. Or Daddy. I wonder if he sometimes comes here for a pint.

"It must be a good five miles to the Carlisle estate," Professor Swift says. "But you're young."

I hadn't expected to find Professor Swift drinking beer on the terrace of the local pub—in fact, it was the very last place I had ever expected to find her.

"Is this your local?" I ask, smiling. I drink eagerly from my beer. Perhaps I should have gotten some water for rehydration purposes. But as Professor Swift just said, I'm young. I can take it.

"It is. I live just down the road," she says.

"It must be so lovely living here." I glance at her, while trying not to gulp down my beer in one go. One won't suffice to quench my thirst. "How long have you lived here?"

"I bought my cottage eleven years ago."

"It must be nice to come home to after a long day dealing with students. Just staring at the river, having a leisurely drink," I muse more than I say.

"You sound as though you're ready to move back home."

When I look at Professor Swift, I'm met by an amused expression on her face.

"Good heavens, no." *That would be much too close to my family.* Just as I think of home, my phone starts ringing and my mother's name appears on the screen. "Please excuse me."

I leave the table before picking up.

"Yes, Mother?"

"Rory, where are you? You've been gone for hours."

"I'm a big girl, Mum."

"You are staying the night, aren't you?"

"Yes, I am."

"Will you be home for supper?" she asks, even though it doesn't really sound like a question.

I pace alongside the river and glance at the pub. "No, I don't think so." One meal at home on a Sunday is more than enough. I said my goodbyes to my brother and his family before I set off on my walk.

"Where are you?"

"In the village. In a pub called The Golden Fleece."

"Hm." A short groan could not possibly sound more disdainful. "Just don't stay out too late. And call George. He'll send someone to pick you up."

"Thanks, Mum." I hang up before she can say anything else.

"Sorry about that," I say before I sit back down. "It was my mother if you can believe it. You'd think I was still a teenager."

"She was probably just worried about you."

"Hm." I realise my own groan sounds just as condescending as my mother's on the phone. Professor Swift's comment makes me wonder if she has children of her own. It certainly wouldn't be unheard of for a lesbian of her age. She could have come out later in life, tried the whole straight marriage thing before realising who she truly was. But I can't ask her any of that. She's not Professor Monohan.

"How are you getting back? You won't be walking, I assume?" Professor Swift asks.

I burst into a little giggle.

"What's so funny?"

"My mother just asked me the exact same question."

"Great minds and all that." Professor Swift doesn't seem too

33

pleased with the comparison to my mother. Maybe she knows her.

"Someone will pick me up." It sounds so posh when I say it like that.

Professor Swift nods. "You'll be summoning your driver." That amused grin is back on her lips.

"If you put it like that." I've found that the best way to deal with any chatter about my family is to be as light-hearted as possible about it. "I couldn't possibly ask you to drive me home." I may have overdone it a bit, I realise as soon as I say the words.

Maybe it's the beer—I don't know how long Professor Swift has been sitting here, knocking them back—but I've actually made her laugh for the first time. Her laugh is much more gregarious than she conducts herself.

"I'm over the limit," she says.

I down the last of my beer—I should have gotten a pint instead of a half. "I'm about to be. Can I get you another?"

She eyes her beer. Her glass is still half-full. "I've had my quota for the day, but thanks."

At the bar, I wisely order some water to go with my next beer.

9

HELEN

While Victoria's inside, Eugenie comes outside to round up the empty glasses from the terrace tables. She gives me a nod, accompanied by a strange smile on her face. Maybe she's surprised I'm still here. I come here often enough, but I'm not usually someone who lingers. Winston the pub dog is at her heels. I give him a quick scratch behind the ears. When I stop, he looks at me with such expectation in his tiny, sparkly eyes, I have to treat him to another round of petting.

Victoria returns with a beer and a large bottle of water. If she wasn't the kind of person who can summon a driver whenever she wants, I probably would have taken her home despite having had two beers. I'd have felt it was my duty.

"I was wondering," Victoria starts. She's not the type to enjoy a beverage in silence. "What with you having lived in Chewford for so long, do you know my parents?"

"You mean Lord and Lady Carlisle?" I can't help but tease her about her family a little.

She nods and doesn't acknowledge my attempt at a joke. They are the Lord and Lady of the manor, after all.

"I certainly know *of* them, but I can't say I run into them on a regular basis. Only when there's something special happening in the village, like the Christmas fête. We're not on speaking terms. Why do you ask?"

"Just curious, really."

"Your mother does a lot of charity work, doesn't she?"

Victoria just nods. She pours herself a large glass of water and drinks it down eagerly. She suddenly looks tired. The long walk must have gotten to her. I usually don't feel this concerned about my students. I usually don't sit outside a pub with them on a Sunday afternoon either.

"Do you need something to eat?" I ask.

She shakes her head. "It's been rather a long day. Spending time with my family can really take it out of me." She smiles sheepishly. "Luckily I don't have to do it too often. It was my brother's birthday."

"You don't enjoy spending time with your family?"

She shrugs, then says, "I don't really know my family and, well, let's just say that, um, Mother wasn't riveted when I told her the subject of my research for the coming four years."

I nod thoughtfully, letting Victoria vent for a bit.

"'Of all the things you could spend time on', were her words, actually," Victoria says. "So no, we're not that close."

"I understand." I must be a good twenty years older than Victoria, but I know exactly how she must feel. Unfortunately, her belonging to a younger generation hasn't automatically made things easier on her. "But you're walking your own path and you're not letting your family influence your professional choices. I applaud that."

"Thanks." Her face lights up. "I really appreciate that, especially today." Her eyes narrow. "Was it difficult for you to come out at the university?"

"No. I've been at Oxford a very long time. First as a student, then to do my DPhil, and finally when I started working as a lecturer. I've seen things change over the years and, well, I'm not *that* old." I send her a grin.

"I didn't mean to imply—" Victoria's cheeks flush a little.

I wave her off. "It's fine. I know people in their twenties think people in their forties are ancient." It hits me again that I'll only be in my forties for a brief while longer, and I definitely don't share that nugget with Victoria.

"You don't look a day over thirty-five, Professor," she says with her usual forward aplomb.

I chuckle with her. Who would have thought I'd enjoy having a candid conversation with one of my students?

"How old are you?" I must have seen her date of birth on her application, but I don't remember.

"Twenty-seven," she says.

"You did two master's degrees, if I remember correctly?"

She nods. "Mainly to escape the pressure to either join the family business or start a family myself. As long as I'm studying, Mother's off my back."

"I do hope you enjoy the process as well." I give her a smile.

"Oh, yes. I really do. I was just saying that…"

"Whether we're close to them or not, no one escapes family pressure entirely." I drain the last of my beer. It's gone lukewarm.

"Especially if you're a Carlisle. Since I was four years old, I've been told that being a Carlisle comes with certain expectations. Falling in love with the same sex wasn't one of them, as you can imagine."

"It's up to you to blaze a new trail then." I hold her gaze for a split second. She has the most remarkably dark pair of eyes. When my glance skitters away, I look at my empty glass. I have a decision to make.

I've chatted to Victoria long enough. "I have to get going. Are you sure you'll make it back home okay?"

Is that a flash of disappointment I see crossing her face?

"Yes, of course." She pours herself some more water. "No problem. It was really lovely chatting with you, Professor."

When we're at my local pub, having her call me Professor does sound a little ridiculous, but I can't waiver on my principles because of one such occasion.

"It was," I concur. "I'll see you tomorrow then. At three."

"Have a nice evening." She's nothing if not polite.

"You too, Victoria." I cast her one last glance before I turn around. "And thanks for the beer." I owe you one, I think, as I make my way home.

❧ 10 ❧

RORY

"You had a beer with Swift?" Jess puts her hands on her hips. "No one ever has a beer with Swift. How did you swing that?"

"My natural Carlisle charm, I guess." On my way to Oxford, I picked up some pastries and we're sitting in the kitchen, devouring them. I left early this morning because I wanted to have enough time to prepare for my upcoming meeting with Professor Swift.

"What was she like?" Jess looks very intrigued. I don't tell her she has a crumb dangling from her chin.

"Very nice. We had a lovely chat, come to think of it."

"It must be because of your research subject," Jess says. "She must have a soft spot for you because you're willing to devote all this time to lesbians."

I chuckle. "Yes, I'm sure that's it."

"I've met most of the students she supervises and they've all only ever said one thing: she's good and thorough and motivational when she has to be, but she's *never* personable."

"It was just a coincidence that I ran into her."

"Was it? How often do you wander away from the Carlisle manor into the village?"

"What are you insinuating?" I huff out a chuckle.

She juts out her bottom lip. "Maybe it wasn't as much of a coincidence as you'd like me to believe."

"Are you saying I walked into Upper Chewford with the deliberate intention of crossing paths with Professor Swift?" I arch my eyebrows.

"I'm just wondering, that's all." She takes another bite of croissant.

"It was definitely a coincidence." I'm not sure why I feel such a strong urge to defend my point. "Would you expect to find Swift having a beer at her local?"

"Sure. Why not? What else is she going to do in Chewford on a Sunday afternoon? Go hunting with the Carlisles?" She's really taking the piss now.

"Fuck off, Jess."

"I'm just winding you up." She wipes the crumbs off her hands. "I have to say, it was rather easy on this lovely Monday morning."

"Now that you've had your fun, I have work to do."

"Oh Christ, so do I. To be on schedule, I have to write about five thousand words today." She buries her head in her hands. "Sarah's going to eat me alive if I don't get her the next two chapters."

"Best get cracking then." I give her an encouraging pat on the shoulder and head to my desk to work on my own research.

Other candidates who have also worked under Professor Swift's supervision have told me what to expect from this first official meeting. I shouldn't worry about it too much. Swift's supposed to be exacting but fair. From what I've been told, she shouldn't be on my case too much during the first few months while I organise my thoughts on my chosen subject and find my way around being a DPhil candidate. All of which is a good thing, because I found it very hard to focus on my research plan this morning.

Maybe Professor Swift doesn't mingle with her students socially for good reason. Because it's a distraction. Perhaps she was more gregarious in her earlier days, but found it didn't lead to very good results.

I do realise these are just first-meeting jitters. Next Monday, I'll already feel much more confident. I knock on her office door and inhale deeply.

"Come," I hear her say.

I enter with a warm smile on my lips.

"Ah, Miss Carlisle. I take it you got home safely yesterday?"

"Without a hitch." It was George himself who picked me up. He probably needed some air after serving a Carlisle family meal.

"Is it hard for you to get by without staff?" She leans back, an actual grin on her face.

"I haven't lived at home for fifteen years—"

"I'm just messing with you. I shouldn't have." She points her finger at a chair. "I apologise. Please, sit."

Even though her joke came from out of the blue, I do quite like it when Professor Swift 'messes with me'. It creates a familiarity I wasn't expecting.

It doesn't take very long for me to tell her what I've prepared and what I intend to do this semester. It's all still rather vague in my head as well. From the two master's dissertations I wrote, I know it will all start coming together once I begin the actual work.

When I'm done, she doesn't ask me any questions at all. She fiddles with a sheet of paper, rubbing it between her fingers. She's fidgeting. I hadn't taken her for the fidgeting type. Then again, I hadn't taken her for the type to have a few beers in her local pub either. Or maybe Jess was right. What else is she going to do in Upper Chewford?

"Hm," she utters after a while. "These first few meetings, I can only give you some general advice, Vic—Miss Carlisle."

"Everyone just calls me Rory," I blurt out.

"Rory," she repeats, then falls silent again. She rolls a pen between her fingers.

"If you don't mind me asking, Professor, is everything all right? You seem a little... preoccupied." I was hardly expecting her to focus all her attention on me, but her energy is totally different from the other times I've seen her. Or maybe she's always like this on a Monday. I only feel a little out of order asking a semi-personal question. After all, she did inquire how I got home yesterday. And we did share a beer.

"I apologise again, Miss Carlisle." For the first time today, she fixes her gaze on me. "It's a personal matter. I really shouldn't allow it to distract me." She straightens her back. "But it does." She huffs out a sigh. "I'll make it up to you next week."

I'm not sure if this is my cue to leave. I also can't help but wonder what's happened in Professor Swift's personal life since yesterday afternoon, when she didn't appear absent-minded at all.

I know that she and Professor Monohan were in a relationship when I was starting my master's, not that there were any outward signs of that. It was just rumours and hearsay. It supposedly ended years ago, so it shouldn't have anything to do with her distraction now.

Maybe she has a partner who came over to her cottage last night... I put a stop to this train of thought. It was what kept me from preparing properly for the meeting this morning in the first place. I should, in fact, count my lucky stars that Professor Swift is as distracted this afternoon as I was all morning.

"Um, okay." I get up to leave. Then a thought hits me. "It's not anything I said yesterday afternoon, is it?"

"Goodness, no." She waves off my comment. "It's nothing for you to worry about, Miss Carlisle." She flashes me a smile, but it isn't as warm as the one she greeted me with. "I'll see you next week."

I refrain from joking that she might run into me at her local again over the weekend. I definitely don't have any plans to go back to Chewford so soon.

I give her a quick nod and exit her office. This meeting didn't go at all as I had anticipated.

❧ 11 ❧

HELEN

For a while, I stare at the door that Victoria Carlisle has just closed behind her. Too long for someone who's running out of time on all fronts. And all of this because of a hobby that's gotten out of hand.

This morning, for some inexplicable reason, I checked my email before my commute. I know from experience that reading emails before writing is always a mistake, but this morning it was extra distracting because of one of the emails I received on my H.S. Barr address. The subject line read:

Professor Helen Swift?

I might be completely wrong, but could it be that H.S. Barr and Helen Swift, Professor of English Literature at Oxford University, are one and the same person?

. . .

Yours truly,
    Andi Morris

I didn't have to google Andi Morris as I very much know who she is—everyone in the UK knows Andi Morris. She's a million-selling traditionally published cozy crime writer. Like me, plus the million-selling and traditionally-published. On the way over, I lost precious time when I could have been dictating my next novel, because I couldn't get that email and its possible ramifications out of my head.

I've always known a day like this would come. A day when I can no longer keep my two identities separate. But I'd always—perhaps foolishly—believed that I would be the one to choose that day. I didn't expect Andi Morris to email me about it.

To make matters worse, I was distracted to the point of negligence during my meeting with Victoria Carlisle. It's so important to set the standard at a first meeting with a new student.

I know it's just another sign—on top of all the others I've been receiving loud and clear—that I can't keep up this double life. I might have given myself another academic year to decide, but I may not even make it through this term.

But first things first. I need to tell someone. Anyone. I need to let the pressure off. I can't cut back my hours at the university to pursue a career I still feel somewhat ashamed of. Because being a cozy crime writer feels like the opposite of being a Professor of English Literature at Oxford University. The two don't go together. I'll have to tell the Faculty Head. But first, I have to tell someone who might be more sympathetic. Maybe Marc or Stacey. Or I could just blurt it out to Josie next time I see her at The Golden Fleece. But no, I can't make it that easy on myself. I know I need to either tell Sarah or Alistair next. Narrowing it down between the two of them isn't that hard.

Sarah is much too judgmental when it comes to fiction. She won't even browse the shelves that hold the commercial genre fiction at a bookstore. She avoided them like the plague when we were still together. She only reads classic or high-brow prize-winning literature, claiming that anything else is a waste of her time and brain power.

Alistair it will be then. I've caught him with a crime novel under his arm before. In fact, I think I once saw him with an Andi Morris book sticking out of his satchel.

~

"I hear you've lowered your standards, Helen," Alistair says as soon as I've sat down. I've invited him to dinner at one of the few places in Oxford where it's unlikely we'll be seen by students.

I give him a puzzled look. I haven't said anything yet. Has he figured it out already? Or worse, did he get approached by Andi Morris as well?

"How do you mean?"

"Sarah told me you were downing pints with Victoria Carlisle in your local yesterday afternoon." He gives me a knowing smile.

"Oh, for heaven's sake. This place." I shake my head.

"I had a chat with young Victoria the other day. She's lovely. There are worse people to drink with." He has the enormous audacity to wink at me. He's not creating the right mood at all for me to share my secret. Of course, he doesn't know that we're here for that reason.

Alistair and I have dinner quite often, although usually not on a Monday evening. I like to go home on a Monday, make the drive, and feel like I've started the week off with a decent word count.

"Oxford's a hotbed of gossip, Helen. It's just the way it is."

He slants his head. "You don't have anything more untoward to share with me, do you?"

"What on earth do you mean?" I'm beginning to think this was a mistake.

"Well, *you know*..."

"No, I don't know." I've known Alistair for years and I adore him, but that doesn't mean he can't royally exasperate me on occasion.

"You don't have a little crush on one of your supervisees?" He quirks up his eyebrows, wrinkling his forehead.

"What?" I peer at him. "Wherever did you get that insane idea?"

"Victoria's a lesbian. She's doing all this lesbian research. You're a lesbian. So many lesbian boxes ticked." He chuckles.

"Christ, Alistair. Sometimes I really wonder how you ever became a member of our faculty."

"I take it a crush is out of the question then." He grins at me.

"Of course it is. Victoria's family happens to live near where I live. She passed by the pub where I was having a drink. She joined me for one. It seemed inappropriate not to. I don't know what you've heard, but that's all there is to it."

"All right, all right, Miss Defensive. I get the picture." He narrows his eyes. "You do have something to tell me. Something urgent. Otherwise you wouldn't break your rigid Monday evening scheduling." His smile is warm now.

"I do, but let's order first." I haven't been able to eat much today. Andi Morris's email messed with my head so much, I could feel it all the way in my stomach.

After we've ordered and are nursing a glass of Chablis, I pluck up the courage to tell him.

"Have you ever heard of a writer called H.S. Barr?" I ask.

He thinks for a few seconds, then starts nodding. "Yes. I think so. I might have read one of his books."

"*His?*"

"Or her, I guess."

"Why would you assume it's a man?"

He eyes me quizzically. "Because we live in a patriarchal society and even though I'm gay, I'm still a middle-aged, privileged, white bastard." He bats his lashes at me.

I have to chuckle. I take a deep breath. "I'm H.S. Barr."

He narrows his eyes even further. "You're H.S. Barr. What does that mean?"

For such a clever man, it can take a good long while before his penny drops. "It means that, in my spare time, I write crime novels under the name H.S. Barr."

He strokes the stubble on his chin. "Well, Helen, I never." He holds up a finger. "Give me a second to process this information."

While he processes, our food arrives.

"This looks scrumptious," I say to break the tension.

"You kept that one hidden very well," Alistair says. "How long have you been writing as... H.S. Barr?"

"Three years, give or take."

He doesn't say anything, just looks at me. He's letting me explain.

"It started after Sarah and I broke up. I really took to it. I loved it. I still love it. But it's all gotten a bit out of hand. I feel like I have a choice to make. Between writing and my work at the university."

"Really?" He doesn't even look at his plate of food. "How many books have you written? Is it even a viable choice?"

I feel like I need to at least start eating, just to set the example. "It certainly could be."

"I'm a little confused, Helen." He does pick up his cutlery now. "Is it lucrative?"

"Cozy mysteries are a big genre in commercial fiction."

"Who's your publisher?"

"I am."

I always knew this would be the most difficult thing to get through any of my friends' heads.

"You are?" he drops his cutlery again and takes a sip of wine.

"I self-publish. Independently."

"I've read some articles about that in *The Guardian*."

"Every single one of them pretty disparaging, I'm sure," I say matter-of-factly.

"Quite." He stares into his wine, then looks up again. "I rather enjoyed your book." He scratches his chin again. "I remember now. It was a cracking read, Helen. I had no idea it wasn't published by some big publisher."

"I take that as a compliment." I truly do.

"So you can just have your independently published books stocked at the local book shop? I believe that's where I bought it."

"You won't find it at the big chain stores, but independent shops do sometimes like to stock books set in the area."

"I should eat this before it gets cold." Alistair seems to have finally noticed his plate.

I take the chance to get some food into my stomach as well.

He's barely swallowed his first bite when he asks, "How many books do you sell? It must be quite a chunk if you're considering leaving your job."

"I'm not considering leaving. Just cutting back. Start by working at the university part-time to be able to manage my time better."

"You didn't answer my question." He grins at me and spears another morsel of fish onto his fork.

"I've sold so many. I can't quite believe it." It's hard to wrap my head around it at times.

"Enough to make up for losing half your salary?" He squints at me, as if a light bulb's going off inside his head. "Enough to buy that Porsche!" he exclaims triumphantly. "I was convinced that was your mid-life crisis."

"I won't deny that it wasn't a little bit of that. I'll be turning fifty soon enough."

"Time for a life change." He nods. "Good for you. Come to think of it, this is all terribly exciting."

"You don't think that writing commercial fiction is... unworthy of an Oxford professor?"

"Unworthy?" He drops his cutlery again. "Where on earth did you get that idea?"

"Some would say it's hardly literature."

"Some? You mean Sarah?" He shrugs. "Who cares what your ex thinks. Screw her."

"I haven't done that in a while."

Alistair bursts out in a chuckle. "Have you been, you know, screwing anyone else?"

"No. I'm far too busy for any of that."

"Christ. That's why you haven't been attending any faculty parties or joining in any of the off-campus fun."

"Yes, sure, that's the reason." We both know I've never been one for 'off-campus fun', whatever that might entail.

"Here I was thinking that all you did in your cottage by the river was contemplate serious literature. All the while, you've been scribbling about unlikely murders in the Cotswolds."

"You're the first person I've told, Alistair."

He brings a hand to his chest. "I'm truly touched." He cocks his head again. "I figured as much, though."

"I'm glad I told you." It doesn't exactly feel like a weight has been lifted off my shoulders, but Alistair's warm reaction is heartening. It makes me wonder why I didn't tell him earlier. I got into my own head too much. I was the one who had the most trouble accepting that what I do is a valid pastime for someone in academia—the most snobbish of environments.

And I imagined my own reaction, before I discovered indie publishing, if any of my colleagues had told me about their own endeavours. I'm probably the most snobbish of all.

But tonight, I made my first baby steps towards acceptance. And a more manageable life.

RORY

"I actually feel old here," I say to Jess.

"You shouldn't have waited so long to start your DPhil," she replies. Jessica is never short of a snappy reply.

"That doesn't exactly make me feel any younger, you know." I drink my beer and it reminds me of last Sunday.

"Come on, Rory. You're twenty-seven. It's still totally appropriate for you to go out with any of these people."

"It's not because it's appropriate that I feel like it." I know I'm pouting for no reason. Maybe because Jess had to drag me to the college's weekly *Tuesgay Drinks*.

"What's with you? You still haven't digested your visit home?" She slants her torso over the high table we're leaning against. "These past few years, as your trusted roommate, I've become somewhat of a connoisseur of all things Victoria Carlisle. Sometimes, I swear I know you better than you know yourself, which is why I made you come tonight instead of leaving you to mope in your room all night."

I have to smile at that. "Cheers, Jess."

"And I have only one mission tonight: getting my bookish friend laid." She waggles her eyebrows, then holds up her glass.

Reluctantly, I clink mine against it. I also shake my head. "That's a bit forward for me. You should know that."

"Perhaps it's the only way to break through your 'Carlisle-ness'." She starts scanning the pub. She does this for a few minutes and only then looks at me again. "I know you don't really have a type, but I believe I have scouted at least three possible candidates for a one-night stand."

"This may be very hard for you to believe, but I don't want a one-night stand." I am secretly a little curious about the three women she has picked out for me.

"You say that now, but you'll thank me in the morning, when all that tension has left your body *and* freed your mind."

"How about we go somewhere else and find someone for you to have a one-night stand with."

She shakes her head firmly. "I'm abstaining until I've caught up on my dissertation."

It's my turn to quirk up my eyebrows. "For real?"

"I want to graduate, Rory. I'm ready for real life to start. I feel like I've been a student forever."

"Is that why you're focusing all your pulling energy on me? To live vicariously through me?" I take a sip of beer.

"Exactly right. Do it for us, Rory. Our apartment hasn't seen action in quite some time."

"The term has only just started. I think that's quite normal."

"Nu-uh." She waves her pint around and some liquid sloshes over the rim. "Stop making excuses and casually glance to your right. A cutie's making eyes at us."

"How can she make eyes at us when I have my back to her?"

"Rory," Jess says forcefully. "I'm here to help so do as I say."

We both burst into a chuckle. Then I do glance to my right.

"She looks like she's still a teenager," I say when I turn back around.

"Yes, well, this is a university, where people in their late teens come to study," Jess states matter-of-factly.

"They need to at least look like they're in their twenties," I say. "And preferably not be undergrads."

"Christ." Jess rolls her eyes. "Maybe you should just go on Tinder. It's much easier to meet all your requirements. We're not talking engagement here, Rory. Or taking her home to meet Mother Carlisle. It's just some fun."

"I can't help who I fancy."

Jess nods. "You used to fancy me."

I give her a look that says, 'not that old chestnut again'.

"What?" She holds out her hands. "I'm younger than you."

"All of eighteen months."

"I'm not seeing a happy ending for tonight with that kind of attitude." Jess looks around again. "Okay, I've spotted someone who looks like she's in her third year at least. Plus, she's cute." She leans over the table again. "Very subtly, turn to your left. She's standing alone at a table in the corner. It's really a shame that a pretty girl like that should stand alone in a corner." She winks at me.

If nothing happens tonight—which is what my gut tells me —it won't be for lack of Jessica's enthusiasm. I wait a beat, then shift my body to the left. I spot the woman immediately. She has short black hair and wide blue eyes and is, indeed, very pleasing to the eye. She also looks more my age than most other people in the pub.

"Not bad." I still have zero inclination to head over to her and strike up a conversation.

"Should I beckon her with my eyes?" Jess grins at me.

"Good luck with that."

"I won't need it. She's headed to the bar and my pint's empty. Your turn to get the drinks." Jess all but shoves me in the direction of the bar.

I expel a deep sigh.

"Come on, Rory. This is your chance. It might be your best one of the night."

"The thing is, Jess... I really, really don't feel like talking to strangers tonight."

I can almost see Jess deflate in front of me, but she quickly regroups. She is my best friend, after all. "How long since you last had a shag?"

I shrug. I don't really keep track. It's not a box that needs ticking at regular intervals for me, especially when I'm single.

"Should I be worried about you?" She waves her empty pint around. "By the way, this is still empty."

"I'll be right back." I head to the bar, avoiding the girl Jess brought to my attention. I glance around. As usual, most of the *Tuesgays* patrons are boys. Still, there's a good female turn-out tonight. Jess was right when she said that all the lesbians come out to play at the beginning of the academic year. "Then they meet someone and don't go out for the rest of the year," were her exact words. They might have made me chuckle, but I also recognised some truth in them.

While I wait my turn, I ponder Jess's questions. Should she be worried about me? What would there be to be worried about? Out of nowhere, at the far end of the bar, I spot a woman with shoulder-length, blonde wavy hair. A flash of something soars through me as I wonder if it's Professor Swift. Then the woman turns around and she no longer bears any likeness to the professor. Something else courses through me. Disappointment? It can't be, although it feels like it.

The barman asks for my order and I lose my train of thought. While I wait for our beers, I glance at the woman again, but she slips out of my field of vision immediately.

"Here you go." Two pints are deposited in front of me. I distract myself by paying for the drinks, then head back to Jess.

"No pulling at the bar?" Jess asks.

"No." Something burns inside me nonetheless. Something I can't place.

"Listen, Rory," Jess says. "That guy over there's been looking in my direction very intently. In fact, if you hadn't returned with the drinks just now, he might have come over."

"Whatever happened to abstinence?" I burst into a giggle.

"That's more your thing, it would appear." Jess sends me a broad smile, then looks over my shoulder.

"Truer words have not been spoken tonight." I'm just happy the focus is off me. I wouldn't know how to withstand more of Jess's questioning.

"Shall I be a good wing-woman and beckon him with my eyes?" I ask.

Jess laughs and nods eagerly.

❧ 13 ❧

HELEN

I still haven't replied to Andi Morris. Why is she interested, anyway? Doesn't she have better things to do with her time than suss out my identity? I need to find out who blabbed—if it's one of the local book stores or whether I've made myself vulnerable on another front. I park my car in front of my house. I've barely made it inside when I get a text.

Sausages are almost ready.

Oh Christ. The barbecue's tonight. I'm in no mood to meet a woman, but I can't back out now. I just need to find a sunnier disposition, which shouldn't be too hard. I managed to get a decent word count in on my drive home and it's a lovely warm autumn evening in Upper Chewford.

I text Stacey back that I'll be there in fifteen minutes. She must have seen me arrive. We live in the kind of street where arriving home from work gets noticed—at least by those with too much time on their hands.

I hurry upstairs to run a comb through my hair and change into something a bit less professor-like—jeans and a colourful blouse instead of a trouser suit.

"You might as well have fun," I tell my reflection in the mirror.

Fifteen minutes later, I arrive at my neighbours with a bottle of wine. Mireille, the mystery guest, has already arrived. At first glance, she looks totally acceptable. I can even see why Stacey would have gotten so excited at the prospect of setting us up.

Introductions are made and Mireille gives me a warm, lingering handshake.

Stacey pours wine while Marc lords over the barbecue.

"I hear you're a professor at Oxford," Mireille starts.

Here we go. With the kind of awe this seems to inspire in so many people, it's a miracle I'm single. It must be me then.

"I am." I take in Mireille's face as Stacey confirms what I've just said, which she loves to do. She would see it as a real feather in her cap if she were to successfully set me up with someone for the long-term.

Mireille's petite in that French way. Her arms are so slim, I'd be afraid to touch them. She has intriguing green eyes and she's wearing a dark green blouse to match them.

I regale them for a while with a few of my much-told Oxford stories, one of them an Alistair classic. While I talk, I feel lighter, less stressed than I've been in a good long while. I'm not sure if it's meeting Mireille, who's very engaging and not the constantly interrupting kind like Stacey, or if it's the fact that I told Alistair what I do as a hobby. Maybe it's a combination of both.

By the time Marc puts a plate of sausages on the table, I'm starting to remember what relaxed really feels like.

While Marc and Stacey run back and forth into the house to get all the necessary condiments and a salad, I feel Mireille's glance on me.

"It's very lovely to meet you, Helen," she says.

"And you," I reply truthfully. "Tell me how you came to live in the Cotswolds."

Mireille's story is interrupted by Stacey and Marc sitting down, after which Stacey, who clearly considers Mireille her new best friend, finishes the story for her. It's the classic tale of someone who has lived in London for too long, got tired of the never-ending rat-race in the concrete jungle, and wanted to take things a lot easier while enjoying nature.

"It rains here as much as it does in London," I joke.

"I've noticed, but it's different here. It doesn't make everything look so gloomy." Mireille's tone is upbeat, but there's also something rather seductive about her voice. It might be the slight hint of French accent.

"Mireille loves to go for long walks," Stacey interjects again.

I used to walk for hours too, as Stacey well knows. That time seems long gone, but the mention of it makes me crave a long walk. The leaves will start turning soon and Upper Chewford and its surroundings will be aglow with autumn colours.

For some reason, I also think about the long walk from the Carlisle manor that Victoria ventured upon last Sunday. I also hear Alistair's words ringing back in my ears. I'm still convinced it was utterly coincidental that she turned up at the pub. What else could it possibly be?

"You moved to the right place for that," I say. "Have you done any of the Cotswold Way?"

The rest of the meal is spent chatting about this and that. Mireille moved to the neighbouring village of Sourton a few months ago, she's truly enjoying her new environment as well as the process of striking up new friendships and, according to my instincts, she's very much on the prowl.

When I get up to leave—I do have an early morning the day after—Mireille accompanies me to the front garden of my cottage, bicycle in hand.

"It's so lovely here by the water," she says.

"I'm very happy here." I glance over the River Ale. It's almost completely dark. The days are getting shorter so quickly now. Soon enough, I'll be sitting by the open fire in The Golden Fleece. Wouldn't it be nice to have someone to spend the upcoming winter with? To sit by the fire with?

"I don't mean to be too forward, but I am still French," Mireille says, a lop-sided smile on her lips. "Would you like to exchange numbers?" She fidgets with the handlebar of her bicycle. "So we can have a chat, just the two of us, sometime?"

"Sure." *Why not?* Mireille is pleasant company. Surely I can find time in my busy schedule for a coffee with a lovely Frenchwoman. She's probably keen to visit Oxford. I could show her around campus. "That would be lovely."

We exchange numbers and when she kisses me lightly on the cheek to say goodbye, I catch her scent, and I'm reminded of how much I've missed someone special in my life.

That night, I sleep like a log. In the span of a week, my prospects have changed somewhat, and I feel hopeful about my future instead of stressed out by all the things I've been trying to juggle. I even manage to not give Andi Morris any more thought than she deserves, although I will have to reply at some point. The question remains whether my answer will be truthful or not.

❧ 14 ❧

RORY

I'm fifteen minutes early for my Monday afternoon meeting with Professor Swift. I check my emails and a message from Professor Fleming has just come in. The subject reads:

A book set in your neck of the woods!

The body of the email includes a link to Amazon. Because the email is from Professor Fleming, I have no qualms clicking the link. I'm quite surprised by what I find. It's not the kind of book you expect an English Literature professor to recommend.

The author is one H.S. Barr and the title of the book is *Chewed Up in Chewford*. I've never heard of the author but of course the village name is very familiar.

The cover screams cozy mystery set in the Cotswolds. I light up at the sight of the bright colours depicting an image of Upper Chewford with all its landmarks—the mill, the church with its tiny patch of grass in front of it and the river running through it.

I have no time to read a guilty-pleasure book like that while working on my research, yet I am very drawn to it. There's still no sign of Professor Swift—it is only ten to three—so I download the sample to my Kindle, which I always carry with me in order to sneak as much reading into my day as possible. This isn't research, but I start reading regardless.

I get so engrossed by the description of Chewford, that I don't hear Professor Swift arrive.

"Anything good?" She's towering over me, glancing at my Kindle.

I snap it shut and stand up. "A book set in Upper Chewford, if you can believe it." I assume Professor Swift would be interested in that, seeing as she knows the village so much better than I do.

She doesn't immediately reply, just stands there staring at me for a moment.

The silence that ensues is a little awkward so I fill it. "Professor Fleming recommended it. I told him my family live in Chewford—"

"Alistair," Professor Swift says curtly.

"Um, yes."

"Come inside." She seems to regroup from whatever it is that has thrown her.

Could it be seeing me? I shake off the thought. I can't even explain why it popped into my mind out of the nowhere—and very inappropriately—like that.

It is good to see Professor Swift again. She's dressed in her usual dark trouser suit—navy today. The pale blue blouse she wears underneath makes the blue of her eyes pop. Her hair is pinned up, leaving her neck exposed. Oh Christ.

Something's beginning to dawn on me.

"Are you all right, Miss Carlisle?" she asks after I've sat down. "It's not the book you were reading, is it?"

"I'm fine." I square my shoulders. I worked hard over the

weekend. I've come to impress. "Have you read it?" I ask. "The book set in Chewford?"

She utters a kind of giggle that I can't make heads nor tails of. "Let's drop that subject, shall we?" Her tone is very insistent. "What have you got for me today?"

I present her with the very detailed chapter outline for my dissertation.

She regards it intently, then looks at me with a smile. "You've given this some serious thought."

"Isn't that what doing a doctorate is all about?" I hold her gaze for a split second. As hard as it is to look away from her gorgeous eyes, it wouldn't be appropriate to keep on staring at her.

"It most certainly is. Most students starting on this journey need a lot more guidance at this stage. You're much more mature than most, it would appear. Not just in age, but..." She stops abruptly.

All the lessons in etiquette I received from a young age never taught me how not to blush when given a compliment by someone I admire. They did teach me how to daintily laugh them off, though. But I don't dismiss this compliment. I came here with the single intention to impress Professor Swift and it looks like my efforts have been fruitful.

"It must be your experience writing two master's thesis," she says.

It must be this irresistible urge I have to please you, I think.

She gives me a few pointers on where I could improve the outline, but nothing that requires a major change. By the time we're done discussing my dissertation, I'm feeling massively chuffed with myself. The fact that I'm so well-prepared makes this meeting go too briskly and hardly any time seems to have passed when it comes to a natural stop—barely twenty minutes after I walked into her office.

"Maybe we should skip next week's meeting," Professor

Swift says. "You don't want me breathing down your neck all the time. You've already proven yourself very independent."

Oh, no! I must rectify this error in her train of thought at once. "That may be so, but I feel a weekly deadline would be very helpful regardless."

She pins her light gaze on me again. I can almost feel it course through me. She isn't on to me, is she? Even before I'm fully on to myself.

"Of course you have the right to see me, Miss Carlisle." She leans back, keeping her gaze on me. I'm really feeling it now. "Who am I to deny you this right? I wouldn't be doing my job if I did."

I want to sigh with relief, but this is where my stoic upbringing comes in handy. "I really appreciate that." My tone is as dry as they come.

"I'll see you next week then." She sends me a small smile. "If you keep going at this pace, you may finish in three years instead of four."

This reminds me of Jess's comment about wanting to live in the real world instead of staying cocooned in this student community we've grown so accustomed to.

"Best not get too ahead of myself." I rise.

She nods curtly and I find myself very unwilling to leave the confines of Professor Swift's office. It feels like I'm seventeen again instead of twenty-seven.

"Let me know what you think of that book." Suddenly, she looks very pleased with herself. I guess I'll have to read it now. In fact, I may go home and read it immediately, just to be able to give her my opinion on it next week, on top of impressing her with the work I've accomplished.

"Will do." I cast one last glance at her, then exit her office. Whatever will I do with myself until next week? Maybe I'll need to let Jess drag me to *Tuesgays* again, just so that I can get this out of my system.

Alternatively, I could find an excuse to go home over the weekend, and head into the village again. I shake my head as I walk through the corridor. If I'm considering spending time with my family just for the off chance of catching a glimpse of Professor Swift, I must have really got it bad.

❧ 15 ❧

HELEN

As soon as Victoria Carlisle leaves my office, I call Alistair, with whom I have a serious bone to pick.

I barely give him the chance to say hello.

"What are you doing recommending H.S. Barr books to my doctorate students? I told you that in confidence, Alistair."

"I didn't tell her you wrote it." He actually sounds offended.

"It doesn't matter what you told her."

"The girl's family lives in Chewford. I just thought it would be fun for her. She's not going to find out it's you, Helen. Why would she? No one has so far."

"I would just really appreciate it if you stopped recommending my book."

"A sale's a sale, isn't it?" He sounds like his usual chirpy self, as though what I'm accusing him of is the most ludicrous thing in the world.

I roll my eyes but of course he can't see. "I know what you can do to make it up to me."

"Whatever you want," he says on an exaggerated sigh.

"I'm meeting Sarah later. I want to tell her about H.S. Barr.

It would be helpful if you could join us. You know what she can be like."

"She's meek as a lamb now that she's met the plumber," Alistair says. "Which also proves she's not as snobbish as you thought."

"Perhaps not when it comes to who she allows into her bed, but surely still when it comes to the kind of books she approves of."

"Then why tell her?" Alistair asks. "Just keep it to yourself."

"No. I want to—*need to*—tell people. It's important to me."

"Okay. Name the place and the time and I'll be there."

Before I break the news to Sarah, I feel like I need to give her something else to focus on. So I decide to share the only other tidbit I have.

"My neighbours set me up with another one of their friends."

Alistair looks at me quizzically. We're at the same restaurant I invited him to last Monday. If I keep this up, I'll be coming here on a weekly basis, informing more and more people about my alter ego.

"And?" Sarah asks.

"She's nice. We exchanged phone numbers."

"*And?*" she asks again.

"We've sent a few text messages back and forth. She may come to Oxford later this week for the obligatory tour."

"Look at that. My two girls. I'm so proud of you."

"Christ, Alistair," Sarah says. "I wish you wouldn't make such a mockery out of us. It's easy enough for you. You and Jack have been together for light-years."

"I'm not making fun of you at all. I was being encouraging. Some might even say sweet," Alistair protests.

"It's all in your tone of voice," Sarah says.

Alistair glances at me. "Maybe today's not the best day to share your other news with Sarah. She's clearly got a humungous stick up her backside this evening. What's wrong? Plumbing issues?"

Sarah ignores him and looks at me. "What other news?"

I asked Alistair for moral support and, of course, this is what he ends up giving me. An opening I can't possibly get out of. I would have liked to have eased it into the conversation a bit more smoothly, but that's not Alistair's style.

I pause too long, because Alistair starts prodding me. "Go on then, Helen."

"I've, um, cultivated a hobby over the past three years."

Sarah draws up her eyebrows.

"Which has turned into somewhat of a second career."

"You've ramped up the suspense enough now," Alistair says. "Just blurt it out, Helen."

"I write cozy mysteries under a pen name." It sounds so very anticlimactic when I say it like this. My words fall totally flat after what Alistair just said.

"You do?" Sarah says.

"H.S. Barr's the name," Alistair says.

"You already know?" Sarah asks him.

"When it comes to the English Department, I am the *only* one to confide in, we all know that." He all but bats his lashes.

We both disregard him. I want to see Sarah's reaction. Her facial expression doesn't really change much.

"What does this second career entail exactly?" she asks.

"It means I spend all my free time writing and publishing a series of books set in the Cotswolds," I explain.

"What do you mean 'publishing'?" There comes the change in her facial expression. It's hard to miss. She looks like she has just bitten into something really sour. "You don't mean *self-publishing*, do you?"

"I very much do."

"I—I'm rather stunned." Sarah narrows her eyes. "The whole image just doesn't compute in my head, Helen. That's not you. You teach early twentieth century literature." She purses her lips for an instant. "I've always known you have dodgy taste in what you read for pleasure, but now you're actually writing it *and* publishing it yourself." She shakes her head, then looks at Alistair. "Are you sure you two aren't playing some elaborate prank on me?"

Alistair pulls his phone out of his bag and fiddles with it. "Look at this." He shows her the screen. I can't see it, but I can imagine what he's showing her.

"Is it even... ethical?" Sarah asks, clearly unimpressed by what Alistair has shown her.

"Why would it not be ethical?" Alistair asks, as though he's my barrister and he needs to argue for me.

Sarah turns to me. "Have you told the Faculty Head?"

"Not yet."

"I just don't understand why you would associate yourself with this whole inferior self-publishing scene. It's so beneath you. If you had to write, couldn't you have found a publisher instead?"

"Aren't you being a little harsh?" I ask.

Sarah's reaction is no surprise to me, but clearly Alistair was wrong when he predicted she wouldn't be so judgmental just because she's in love.

"Maybe," Sarah says. "But you're a highly regarded professor of English Lit at Oxford. You can't just go self-publish some books on your own."

"Nowhere in my contract with the university does it say I can't." I'm so glad I told Alistair first. I try to remember the lovely things he said to me. Maybe Sarah just needs to get over the shock.

"It just doesn't feel right to me." She's nothing if not

extremely straightforward about it.

"Darling," Alistair says. "Helen hasn't told you the crux of the whole thing yet. Her books are selling so well, she's considering going part-time at the university."

"What? You can't be serious, Helen. That will be the end of your career. We all know you're next in line for the head's job."

"Well then, maybe you'll be next in line instead of me." I look Sarah straight in the eye.

"But how can you give up what you've built all these years?"

"How?" Sarah's reaction doesn't rattle me as much as I had expected, because I still have Alistair's words in my back pocket and—it occurs to me now—it was rather lovely to catch Victoria Carlisle reading my book this afternoon. "Because I love it. Because it's the most fulfilling thing I've ever done. Because it suits me. For all of these reasons. I don't want to be head of the department and work even more. In fact, I'm quite ready for a change of career."

"Maybe you've been around millennials too long," Sarah says, "because you're beginning to talk like one."

"Okay, ladies. Time out," Alistair says. "Let's all take a deep breath here." He actually brings his hands up and shows us by example how to take said breath.

"Sarah, why don't you read one of Helen's books and save your judgment for after," he says.

Sarah looks as though Alistair has suggested she date men again.

"She doesn't have to read one of my books, Alistair." Sarah obviously needs some time to process—perhaps in the company of her plumber.

"I've read one and I'm halfway through the second now," Alistair says.

I glance at him and can't suppress a smile. He's mouthy and at times incendiary, but he's also just a really lovely man—and the best of friends to have. I've already forgiven him for recommending my book to Victoria Carlisle.

"Fine, I'll read it," Sarah says. "But don't go expecting rave reviews from me. You know that's not what I usually read."

"Maybe Joan will like it," Alistair says.

Sarah's face lights up at the mention of her name. "She just might, actually."

"That's settled then. Now tell me, when can we meet the no-doubt lovely Joan?" he asks.

"Soon." Sarah looks at me again. Her glance is much warmer than before, soft even. "Maybe we can triple-date and you can bring Mireille."

I hold up my hands in defence. "Moving a bit too fast there. We've only met once."

"When is she coming to Oxford?" Sarah asks.

"I'm not telling you because I don't want to risk running into you and Joan."

"Touché!" Alistair says.

The mood has brightened and, despite Sarah's tense but predictable reaction, I feel lighter and more optimistic once again. And who knows, things might actually work out with Mireille.

16

RORY

I'm going back and forth between reading the book Alistair recommended to me and daydreaming about Professor Swift when my light is blocked by someone standing next to me.

Jess glares at me with her hands on her hips. "Spit it out, Rory," she says. "You've been back from Chewford a week. This can't still be Mother Carlisle's vibes dampening your mood."

"What are you on about?"

"You're doing this thing that you sometimes do... a communication freeze. Like I don't exist anymore."

I put down my Kindle. "You must be grossly exaggerating because I'm sure I've been my usual communicative self." I flash her a smile.

"According to you perhaps, but not according to your best friend and roommate." She sits on the window sill. "I know when Rory Carlisle has a bug up her bum and I also know that telling me all about it is the only thing that will make you feel better. Unless it's something I did, but I've been an angel, so I really wouldn't know what that could be." She beams me an angelic smile.

Obviously, nothing gets past Jess. But how can I tell her something I don't even want to admit to myself? Something so foolish and pubescent the mere thought of it makes me burn with embarrassment. Yet there it is again. The image of Professor Swift in my head. It's as though it's lodged there and no matter how many other thoughts I try to cram into my brain, she just remains stuck there, taking up valuable space. Maybe I do need to talk about it. Take away its power by putting it into words.

"It's nothing, really. I mean it's really very silly."

"Might a G&T, expertly mixed by yours truly, help?"

It's the middle of the afternoon, but I nod eagerly.

Jess's expert style of mixing consists of nothing more than dumping some ice, a splash of tonic, and a good measure of gin into a tall glass.

When she hands it to me, I take a big gulp first.

"Before I say anything, you have to promise you won't laugh."

We've moved to the sofa and we sit facing each other, legs drawn up, drink in hand.

"Is it that serious?"

"No, it's not serious at all," I admit. "It's silly, so I know you'll just laugh at me." But perhaps that's exactly what I need. For Jess to have a good laugh at my expense.

"You can't keep me in suspense much longer, Rory. I'm dying here."

"I'm not even sure I can get the words past my lips, that's how ludicrous it is."

"Do you need me to guess?" Jess paints on a smirk. "You know I love a good guessing game."

I shake my head. "You'll never guess."

"Take another sip and just blurt it out then. Close your eyes if you must."

I drink again and it makes me feel like an overly hormonal

teenager sneaking a drink with my best friend in the middle of the afternoon and getting ready to confess to a crush.

"It's Professor Swift," I say while staring into my glass. "I can't seem to get her out of my head." I giggle like an infatuated schoolgirl. "I told you it was too stupid for words."

"I don't see what's so stupid about that." The serious tone of Jess's voice surprises me.

I glance up at her. She does have the beginnings of a grin on her lips.

"It *is*. It's completely and utterly ridiculous. It's a teacher crush. It's the sort of stuff that occupies the mind of unstable teens. I'm twenty-seven. And she's not even my teacher."

"Exactly. So don't just shrug it off as a teacher crush. Besides, Swift's a bit of a fox. She and Sarah made the most dashing couple." Jess leans over and lowers her voice, as though it's not just us in the apartment. "You know I once asked Sarah why they split up." Her tone is conspiratorial.

I'm all ears.

"She didn't really give me an answer, unfortunately."

"You have to promise you won't tell anyone, Jess. Especially not Monohan. Or Fleming."

"Who do you take me for? I won't tell a soul, Rory. Your secret's extremely safe with me." She takes a good gulp from her drink, then puts her glass away. "The real question is, what are we going to do about this?"

"There's nothing to be done but wait for it to pass."

"I strongly disagree." Jess shuffles a bit closer. "There are quite a few options here."

"What are you talking about?" I stare into Jess's eager face.

"Supervising professors dating their doctorate students is not unheard of, you know. Admittedly, it's somewhat frowned upon..."

I shake my head. "Now you're the one being silly."

"It's human nature, Rory. Oxford is like a miniature society, like a microcosm. Inevitably, people will be drawn to each other and, well, shenanigans will ensue."

"No." I won't even entertain the thought.

"Let me have a think." She taps a finger against her chin. "Argh, I can't give you any examples off the cuff, but I'm sure there have been loads of professors who got it on with their students. There's just no other way. Let me do some research."

"The only research you should be doing is for your dissertation."

"I'm well past the research stage. I just have to write the bugger now." She expels a deep sigh. "What a pain in the arse that's proving to be."

"I won't have you procrastinate like this."

"Believe me, I need the distraction." She reaches for her glass on the coffee table. "Anyway, my dissertation is not what we're discussing. I was just telling you about your options, one of them being that... you seduce her." I have no idea how Jess is able to keep a straight face.

"These," I lift up my glass, "are strong, but not that strong. Yet it seems to have gone to your head already."

"The other option is, indeed, that you put her out of your mind, which won't be easy since she'll be your supervisor for the next three years. You'll have regular meetings with her. All that time alone in Swift's office." She quirks up her eyebrows and looks at me as though there's only one possible conclusion.

"It's just a crush. It'll pass."

"Will it?" She cocks her head. "Think of those intriguing blue eyes. The intensity of her stare. Plus, she seems quite fit for her age."

I burst into a chuckle. Jess chuckles with me.

"Do you know how old she is?" Jess asks after we've calmed down a bit.

I shake my head.

"Shall we google her extensively?" she offers.

I shake my head even more fervently. "I'm not going to..." This is an even harder word to get past my throat. "Seduce her or google her or anything like that. I'm just going to act my age and let it blow over."

"I'd have never taken you for a cougar lover, Rory. Hm, maybe that's why things didn't work out between us."

"Things didn't work out between us because you realised you like men more than women."

"Hm, there's that." Jess narrows her eyes. "Just don't ever forget you're a catch, Rory Carlisle. Swift would be lucky to have you. In fact, she should be honoured that you have a crush on her."

"But she will never, ever find out."

"Of course she won't." Jess makes the locked-up sign over her lips. "These are well and truly sealed."

"I think my best option is to try *Tuesgay* again," I reluctantly admit.

Jess draws her lips into a pout. "Let's just set you up that Tinder profile, Rory. I don't think *Tuesgays* are your scene." She winks at me. "Let's do it right now and find some cougars for little Rory."

I have to laugh again. It was a good decision to tell Jess. Now it's no longer this unspoken thing festering inside of me. And I should be able to get over it much quicker.

17

HELEN

Another week passes before I invite Mireille to Oxford. The beginning of the academic year is always hectic and it takes a while before I find some room in my schedule. At least that's how I explain it to her—and to Stacey, who accosts me almost every evening as I emerge from my car. Early retirement may sound appealing, but clearly, it leaves some people with too much time on their hands, my neighbour being one of them.

I have been very busy, so it's not that I lied to Mireille about that. But the plain truth is that I simply haven't thought about her that much. The urge to see her again subsided rather quickly after our first meeting. But I have to give it a chance. I can't let my schedule destroy the chance of a love life, even if it's only a tiny glimmer of one at the moment.

I meet her outside Magdalen College and take her up to my office first.

She looks pretty ravishing in a flowery blouse and with her hair pinned up. It strikes me again how absolutely tiny she is. When we walk side by side, I feel like a giant compared to her.

I haven't told Sarah or Alistair that Mireille is visiting today. I don't need them breathing down my neck while I'm trying to get to know a woman.

"Can we sit for a second?" Mireille says, as soon as I've closed the door of my office behind us.

"Sure. Cup of tea?"

She nods and I flick on the kettle. A rather uncomfortable silence hangs in the air while I wait for the water to boil. Mireille glances around my office.

"Lovely space. Very... professorial," she says. Her gaze rests on the door leading to a small room where I sometimes spend the night when I don't feel up to the commute—or if I've had a few too many after work.

I pour us both a cup of tea.

"It's quite a long drive up here," Mireille starts. "So I've had ample time to consider whether I should tell you this or not. But I value honesty above anything else, so in the end it was a no-brainer."

I'm nothing if not intrigued. What on earth does she mean? I just nod. The tea's too hot to drink from yet.

"It was really lovely meeting you at Marc and Stacey's and I'm very happy to be here with you today." She glances around the room again. "I'm honoured that you would take me on a private tour of Oxford. It's a real privilege..."

This is beginning to feel like a break-up conversation, except there's nothing between us to break up from.

"But you should know, Helen, that last weekend I met someone. Online. On Tinder of all places. It's very early days, but she and I really hit it off."

I'm not sure what I'm supposed to say to that. The small glimmer of hope at reigniting my flailing love life is immediately dashed. Maybe I will have to join Sarah and Joan at the 'lesbian gathering' where they met. Or maybe they don't go anymore now that they've found each other.

"I see," I utter eventually. "Have you thought about how you're going to tell Stacey?" The best thing I can do right now is crack a joke.

Mireille smiles. "We have choir practice tonight. I'll break the news to her then."

I'm not exactly hurt by this—how could I be?—yet it stings a little regardless. It's more a blow to my ego than anything else. Another woman is clearly more interesting than me. She's probably more available as well. Maybe I gave off a certain vibe at the barbecue.

"I'm very happy for you. That you've found someone."

"I didn't want to tell you via text message. And I really did want to see you again, Helen. But I also didn't want to create any expectations."

"I appreciate your honesty." In the end, I figure it will save me more precious time. It pains me somewhat that I mentioned Mireille to Sarah and Alistair, however. But they should be old and wise enough not to make too big a deal out of it. *Yeah right.*

We sip our tea in silence. How do you continue a conversation after something like that? I can only revert to small talk now. And to think I'd even contemplated telling her about my H.S. Barr alter ego. If I'm going to be comfortable with it, I need to be able to tell possible love interests. Not just as a conversation topic and as a means to open up, but to manage expectations about the time I have to spend with someone new.

As I put down my cup and saucer, I make the decision there and then to tell the head by the end of the month and scale back my hours the next term. Not only to have more time, but also to have a chance, however small, of something resembling a love life. Things with Mireille might have been doomed from the very start, but she has given me a glimpse of what it can feel like again. The thrill of anticipation. The wonder of getting to

83

know another person. One more winter alone is all I have in me, I reckon.

"Shall we go for that tour then?" I ask.

❧ 18 ❧

RORY

I've been in the Bodleian Library for hours and my eyes are beginning to hurt. I've not been able to unearth any reference to lesbian characters in the portion of English Literature I devoted my time to today. I didn't expect to. I was just keen to spend some time in this gorgeous library. Just sitting here makes me feel smarter already.

It hasn't really helped me get my mind off Professor Swift, however. I'm beginning to think Jess was right. Because now my research is making me think of her as well. The connection is easy enough to make, not only because she's my supervisor, but also because of the subject of my dissertation.

On top of that, the book Professor Fleming recommended to me, the one set in Upper Chewford, features a lesbian detective and it has made me wonder about the scope of my research. Where to draw the line and should I draw a line at all? But if I don't, where will it end?

This is definitely something I should discuss with my supervisor, and that's how my thoughts always end up fixed on Professor Helen Swift.

I put the books I was perusing back and make my way out.

Even though it's a grey day, the light outside is bright compared to the dimly lit library and I have to blink a few times before my eyes adjust.

My phone buzzes in my back pocket as I make my way across the grounds. Probably a Tinder message. I should really switch off the notifications because they're starting to bug me. So far, it has proven to be a disappointing experience. Some of the women I have a match with seem perfectly lovely, but my interest level in anyone else but Professor Swift is disappointingly low.

I stop to look at my phone. It's a text from Jess asking me to meet her at the pub at the end of our street. She has, once again, managed to forget her keys. The trade that pub gets just because Jess often forgets her keys.

When I look up from my phone, two figures are approaching, one of which I recognise immediately. A flash of heat courses through me. I tuck my hair behind my ears and burst into a spontaneous smile. Is it Professor Monohan she's with? No, the person walking beside Professor Swift is much shorter.

They're quickly approaching now. I try to look casual.

"Ah, Miss Carlisle," Professor Swift says. "Working hard as usual?"

"I have to, otherwise my supervisor would be on my case," I blurt out. I even manage a smile.

"Mireille, please meet Victoria Carlisle, one of the doctorate students I supervise," Professor Swift says.

"How do you do," the petite woman says. It sounds very formal and she has an accent I can't immediately place.

"Nice to meet you, Mireille." I quickly shake her hand.

"Victoria's researching lesbian characters in English Literature," Professor Swift says. I can't believe she's calling me Victoria.

"Sounds like quite a job," Mireille says.

I briefly wonder if I should ask Professor Swift now about

what I was just thinking about, but it doesn't seem like the time or place. I'll send her an email later. Perhaps ask for an extra meeting. Oh yes, that definitely sounds like a plan.

"It's something I'm very passionate about," I hear myself say, even though my mind is already busy envisioning the extra meeting.

"I'd love to read your paper once it's done," Mireille says.

Why is this Mireille so interested in my dissertation?

Oh. I give her a good once-over.

"I've only just started," I say. Is that a spark of jealousy burrowing its way through me? Simply because Professor Swift is walking around campus with another woman who *might* be a lesbian? I really have to get a grip.

"You continue with your work then," Professor Swift says. "I'm showing Mireille the library."

They stand a few feet from each other and there are zero indications of romantic involvement between them, yet I can't shake the feeling that something's going on.

"Have fun," I say and quickly head to the pub. I hope Jess has ordered me a drink already.

"It's getting out of hand," I say dramatically when I'm perched on a barstool next to Jess. "It's like I can't control it."

"Of course you can't control it, which is why you need to get it out of your system. You need to replace these unrequited feelings you have for Swift with something else. Starting with a good rush of endorphins."

"I might go for a run later," I say dejectedly.

"I'm not talking about a run, Rory." She waggles her eyebrows and that can only mean one thing. Jess holds out her hand. "Give me your phone."

"What? No."

"Come on. I'll find you a match." She moves her fingers as though she can magically beckon my phone into her hand by doing so. "I won't swipe right without your permission, I solemnly swear."

"No."

"Rory, we have to nip this in the bud. Unrequited... lust can be a dangerous thing if left unchecked. Remember Simon?"

"Simon has made sure I will never forget him."

"You don't want Swift to remember you in that way." She wiggles her fingers again. "Besides, I just read this article about how playing Tetris after a traumatic event can help with PTSD. Not that it's really comparable, but running into Swift with her possible lady friend was your traumatic event and some serious Tindering will be your Tetris. Come on, there's nothing like a good dose of hope to get you over something disappointing."

"The point is that it shouldn't be disappointing. I shouldn't be jealous. I shouldn't even feel this way." I sound so unlike myself. It's like a younger version of myself has taken over my current personality.

"The point is also that you *do* feel all those things so let's do something about them."

Because I have nothing to lose, I hand Jess my phone.

"Here we go." She starts scrolling. "How about we change the parameters a little. Widen the area and broaden the age range, just a fraction."

I just shrug.

A few seconds later, she starts showing me pictures of possible dates. I shake my head at all of them—simply because they're not Professor Swift.

"Come on, Rory," Jess says. "It's not going to work if you say no every single time. Look at this one. She looks very sophisticated." She shoves the phone in front of me.

I do a double-take. It can't be. I examine the picture more closely.

"Either I'm losing my mind or that's the woman I just saw with Swift."

"No way." Jess looks at the picture. "The plot thickens!"

"You don't think... they met on Tinder?" I just can't picture it. Professor Swift scrolling through images of women like that.

"Much stranger things have happened, Rory." She grins at me. "Shall I swipe right and see what happens?"

"What? No, of course not. I just met her. She's going to recognise me. She'll tell Swift."

"Is she going to tell Swift she's still scrolling through Tinder while they're dating?"

"*Might* be dating." My voice shoots up. "I have no idea what's going on between them."

"This is your chance to find out."

I shake my head. "I can't do that."

"It's just a swipe, Rory. Not a commitment. A chance to chat. You can always still say it was a mistake." She pauses. "Besides, if she were to tell Swift, she'd have to explain why she's looking for women under thirty."

"Absolutely no way." I hold out my hand. "Give me back my phone, please."

Jess tilts her head. Her lips are drawn into a pout. She deposits the phone in the palm of my hand. Jess must have realised that what she was proposing crossed far too many lines. I'm just glad I didn't get too caught up in the moment with her.

"How do you plan to get over this then?" she asks.

"A problem came up during my research," I say, avoiding Jess's glance. "I need to make an extra appointment with Swift."

Jess's lips spread into a grin, then she starts nodding.

"Don't," I say sternly, "even think about high-fiving me right now."

❧ 19 ❧

HELEN

"It's very readable," Sarah says. "I honestly had trouble putting it down." Her words sound as though she wants to give me a compliment, but her demeanour says otherwise.

"But?" I ask.

"I don't know, Helen." Sarah has popped into my office to tell me this. "What does it say about the human condition?"

"Excuse me?"

"I can see why a book like that would be fun to write—and read, but..." She glances around nervously. Sarah has never been good at communicating difficult things. I've never made it easy on her either and I don't plan to now. Because this shouldn't be so difficult. She's just being her usual snobbish self. Come to think of it, it does bear some resemblance to how she used to behave while we were together. How she judged us as a couple, because, for the longest time, her brain refused to parse that we were two women in love, two women who were happy being with each other.

"I'm all ears." I paint on an expectant smile.

"It's hardly Literature with a capital L, is it?"

"Does it have to be?" I snicker inwardly. Sarah couldn't be

more herself right now. At least she's not pretending to be someone she's not any more.

"It's a challenge for me to reconcile a book like that with the Helen Swift I know," she says. "With what you teach and who you are."

"There can be many sides to one person. I'm not just a professor of English Literature. I'm so much more than that. Just like you."

"I really liked the main character." Sarah narrows her eyes. "The physical description reminded me of someone."

"Oh, really. Who would that be?" It's so easy to predict what she's going to say next. There might even be a tiny bit of truth in it, but I will never admit to that. Not to Sarah.

"Me?" It's more a question than a statement.

"My characters are never based on just one person," I say. "They're a combination of all the different people I meet."

Sarah nods as though she doesn't believe a word I've just said. If she likes to believe that DI Orla Parish is based on her, that's fine with me.

I'm distracted by the sound of an incoming email. I briefly glance at my screen, which I usually wouldn't do, but I could use a break from Sarah's judgment—even though I know this is her way of trying to be nice.

It's an email from Victoria Carlisle and just seeing it come in, her name in bold letters on my screen like that, shifts something inside me. Or maybe it's just a residue of annoyance from explaining that the human condition doesn't have to be touched upon in every single work of fiction ever written.

The subject of the email is *Scope of research*. I have to keep myself from clicking on it straight away. I briefly wonder what Victoria thought when she ran into Mireille and me the other day. Did she think we were together? She could have thought a number of things and I don't even know why I'm asking myself such a question. It has no relevance. I focus my attention back on Sarah.

"Something important?" she asks.

I just shake my head.

"You just had the funniest look on your face, Helen. Not really a smile, but definitely not a frown either." She cocks her head. "Did Mireille email you?"

"Mireille? No." *Here we go*.

"I know she was here, Helen."

"Ah yes, nothing that happens on this campus gets past Professor Monohan's eagle eyes." I chuckle. "That's why you're really here. Is that why you're pretending you liked my book? So you can give me the third degree about Mireille?"

"I actually take offence at that. I really did enjoy your book. It's like... a really lovely snack. A choc ice when all you've been having is green salads."

It's now my turn to cock my head. I presume there's a compliment buried in there somewhere. I suppose I can indulge her curiosity now.

"If you must know, Mireille's met someone else," I say. While I wait for Sarah's reply, my eyes are drawn to Victoria's email again. Her dissertation is something I'm very invested in personally and I wonder what she has to say about the scope of her research.

"How is that even possible?" Sarah asks. "You just met her."

"You know what they say. You wait ages for a bus to come along and then all of a sudden there are two in a row. I guess the other bus was more attractive than me."

"What are you doing comparing yourself to a bus?" Sarah leans forward. "I'm sorry, Helen. Are you upset?"

I shake my head. "There's nothing to be upset about. She was playing the field and I guess I waited too long. She was very apologetic about the whole thing. You know how it is when you meet someone you really like—as opposed to meeting someone you might possibly like."

Sarah pulls her lips into a satisfied grin. "I do. Speaking of —" She pauses abruptly.

"What?"

"I was going to invite you and Alistair to have dinner with me and Joan, but I just realised my timing is a little insensitive."

"Says the woman who just inquired about the human condition in my book." I offer her a warm smile. Sarah's insensitivity is hardly new to me. "I'd love to meet Joan."

"I'll set it up." She slants backwards again. "So, tell me, how many of these books have you written?"

"I've published three. The fourth is almost ready for publication, and I'm in the middle of writing the fifth."

"Blimey... wherever do you find the time?"

"Here and there." I won't go as far as to admit to Sarah's face that writing the books was instrumental in getting me over our break-up.

"And you're making enough money off these books to consider working part-time?"

"Not quite yet, but I've never been a big spender. I have enough saved to allow me to work part-time here while exploring the option of writing more books. To see where it could lead."

"I'm doing my best to understand, Helen. That you would give this all up." She glances around my office as though it's the most ornate room in Buckingham Palace.

"I'm turning fifty in a few months."

"Ah." She nods as though she only now really understands. "The Big Five Oh. I've been there."

"I've been a professor for a long time; I don't have to be one for the rest of my life." I scan her face to make sure I can say what I'm about to say. "And writing... even though it's a rushed affair almost all of the time and I have to squeeze it in here and there, it just makes me feel so alive. So connected to something I never knew I had in me. To put it very simply, it makes me feel bloody good, Sarah. Better than I've felt in a very long time."

"Who am I to argue with that?"

"You're my ex who cares for me and is looking out for me." My lips spread into an involuntary smile.

"You should go for it then. We're always telling our students to follow their dreams, why shouldn't we do the same?"

"Are we?" I look into Sarah's dark eyes. "I never advise a student to follow their dreams. What am I? American?"

We both chuckle at this long-standing joke we have between us.

"Joan's reading your book now. She's really into it. She'll be super chuffed to meet you."

"Tell her I can't wait to meet her either." I'm glad Sarah stopped by. I'm glad I told her. Next step: the Faculty Head. I hope.

❧ 20 ❧

RORY

My next regular meeting with Professor Swift is on Monday, yet I managed to get her to see me on Friday afternoon. I could tell myself all sorts of stories about that, but I refuse—for my own good. I could, however, swear that the little voice in my head, admonishing me for feeling the way I do, sounds exactly like my mother's.

Heart beating in my throat, I knock on her door.

"Miss Carlisle, come in." I guess she only calls me Victoria in front of possible love interests.

I'm glad to be sitting down. I shouldn't be this nervous. After all, I am here for a reason.

"Tell me what's on your mind." Professor Swift flashes me the warmest smile. It could be my imagination—and it probably is—but I think I detect a twinkle in her eye. Maybe she is on to me.

No. I banish the thought from my head. Even if she is, she must be used to it. There must have been a number of students that have had a crush on her over the years. Maybe she has developed a sure-fire way of detecting even the slightest whiff of a crush on her. Or maybe she's just become indifferent to them. *Get a grip, Rory!*

"Well, uh—" It takes me a few seconds to gather my thoughts. It's always such an assault on my senses to come face to face with her—and such a brusque reminder of why I feel the way I feel.

Professor Swift seems to have time and patience in spades this afternoon.

"That book set in Chewford is actually why I'm here. The main character, a Detective, is a lesbian. I did some digging but I couldn't find anything about the author and there's no mention of a publisher, so I assume the book is self-published." I glance at Professor Swift. This is my subject and this has nothing to do with my infatuation, so this is the only opportune moment I have to really study her face—without it making me feel too awkward.

Her mouth is pulled into a grimace and she suddenly looks like she's quickly running out of patience.

"What I wanted to discuss with you is whether I should include commercial genre fiction in my research or stick to literary fiction. I did some quick research and there are literally thousands of commercial fiction books—self-published and with legacy publishers—featuring lesbian characters, so I'm not sure."

Professor Swift nods slowly, as though she's pondering my question deeply.

"What did you think of the book?"

"It was a nice change from all the early twentieth century tomes I've been slogging my way through, I can tell you that." I mirror her nod—I can't help myself. "And the author knows much more about Upper Chewford than I do. It was actually rather educational. It makes me want to go home more." I catch myself in a bit of a lie there. The only reason I'd go home more often is not for the green splendour of the Cotswolds countryside, but for another chance encounter with Professor Swift.

"Maybe I should give it a go myself then," she says, a small smile on her face.

"I should thank Professor Fleming for recommending it to me," I say just to keep the conversation going. Upper Chewford is the only thing that connects us outside of the university.

"Your question is a valid one," Professor Swift says. "It's good that you're asking it now." She rests her magnificent gaze on me for a fraction of a second longer than I had expected and I can feel my cheeks go red. Oh, bugger. If she notices at all, Professor Swift is very professional about it. "Self-published books are appearing in ever greater numbers these days. What's your reasoning for excluding them?"

I stare at her for a moment, collecting my thoughts. "It seems that most self-published fiction falls into the genre category."

"So you want to exclude genre?" Swift taps a pen on her desk for a moment. "Narrowing your original proposal?"

For a few minutes, we bat ideas back and forth. Swift has a way of cutting to the core of what I'm aiming at—maybe even before I've formulated it myself. She's good. This is one of the reasons I wanted her as my supervisor. Her incisive mind—and subject knowledge. That she's now consuming my thoughts in other ways is a bonus.

"How about we both think about it over the weekend," she says, "and compare notes on Monday?"

"Okay." It is Friday afternoon, after all.

"I hope you weren't planning to enthusiastically dive into the world of commercial fiction with lesbian characters over the weekend."

I shake my head. "I was planning to go home, actually," I say, sounding very keen, even though I have zero plans of doing so. "There's a description of an old chapel in the Chewford book. I wanted to see if it's real or made up."

"It's real," Professor Swift says without hesitation.

"Guess I don't have to go home anymore then." Again, it might be my imagination, but I feel a shift in the air. Something has changed. I can't put my finger on what it might be—apart from wishful thinking on my part. Either way, it's enough for my brain to take a back seat and my runaway mouth to take over. "Although I did rather enjoy that drink we had at the pub last time."

"Did you now?" She rests her gaze on me briefly, then looks away, out of the window.

I nod. I'm not sure what's going on. Whatever it is, it seems to have been ignited by the mention of that Chewford book. I rack my brain for something else I can say about it, just to prolong the atmosphere in this office right now. I come up empty. All I can think of is sitting across from Professor Swift outside the pub. Is that when this started happening to me? When I caught a glimpse of her off-guard? Of what she's like beneath her professional veneer?

"If you happen to be in the area, you might find me in the pub on Sunday afternoon, say around four o'clock," she says.

I swallow hard, my mind racing.

"It could replace our Monday meeting," she says matter-of-factly. "And maybe you shouldn't walk all the way from your family's house this time." The grin that she sends me is one that I already know I'll be dreaming of for weeks to come.

"I'll be there." I don't care that I'll have to spend time with my family. I can just drive to the pub from Oxford on Sunday afternoon. That sounds like a much better plan.

"Very well."

I get up. As much as I want to linger in Professor Swift's

office, I also want to leave before she changes her mind. "I'll see you then." As I exit, I conclude that she and Mireille must not have plans for Sunday afternoon—if they're even together.

HELEN

On Sunday afternoon, when I'm my usual wiped-out self, I wonder what on earth came over me when I asked Victoria to meet me at the pub. I only have to glance at my laptop to know the answer to that.

I want to tell her. I want to see her reaction when I confide in her that I wrote *Chewed Up in Chewford*.

It's a gauge for other people's reactions. I'm her supervisor, which makes me her superior, so this should be the easiest time I have telling anyone. But she is a scholar of serious literature—all of it having something very profound to say about the human condition—so her reaction does matter. Something about her also tells me that my secret will be safe with her. She's a serious young woman, that's written all over her.

But really, my asking her to meet me at the pub happened very quickly. It certainly wasn't premeditated. I went with my gut, which is also exactly what I did when I started writing. I suppose I just really want to tell someone else before I tell the head. I need another practice round. And now that I've had a chance to think about it, I also want to advise Victoria to not include genre fiction in her research. It would turn it into a never-ending task.

It's only three when I arrive at the pub, but I really need to get away from my laptop. I've had no relaxation at all so far this weekend. Working from home has that kind of guilt-inspiring effect on me. Whenever I'm idling, I feel like I need to be doing something because time is always running out.

If I'm going for a drink anyway, I might as well do it with a DPhil student I find more interesting than most. Also, if I'm not alone, Marc can't stop and ask me impertinent questions about Mireille on his wife's behalf.

The fact is that I rather enjoyed having a drink with Victoria Carlisle. She's smart and well-spoken and we have quite a few things in common. And Sarah and Alistair have drinks with their doctorate students all the time. Maybe it's time I followed their example, seeing as I'm so keen to change things up in my life. This is a good start. Even more practice for later.

It's too cold to sit outside. The weather hasn't been very tourist-friendly, so my favourite table inside is free.

Next Monday I'll be running my very last pub quiz here, although I have already been thinking about taking it up again next term, if I do start working part-time at the university.

I nod at my hairdresser who's ordering drinks at the bar and it makes me run a hand through my hair. I should make an appointment at A Cut Above soon—I shouldn't wait until next term for that.

I glance out the window. It's drizzling outside and I hope Victoria drives here today. She looks like a sensible enough woman. I imagine her walking down from the Carlisle manor, the rain against her face, her one-of-a-kind mouth pulled into a grimace. I shake the thought off because I find it a little inappropriate.

As if I summoned her by the power of thought, Victoria walks by the window. I check my watch. She's early.

When she walks in, she looks around. Her face lights up when she spots me.

"I'm a little early," she says apologetically, as though it's a nuisance. "I allowed more time because of the weather. I know how the roads can get on a Sunday when it's like this. But I breezed through." She glances at my glass of wine. "Can I get you another one of those?"

I rise. "I'll get it." I can't have my students buying me drinks all the time. "You sit down." I briefly smile at her. "What would you like?"

Victoria looks flustered by my question. "Same as you," she says after a beat.

"I don't mean to pry, Helen," Josie says as she pours the wine. "That girl looks so familiar, but I can't place her. Care to fill me in?"

I'm taken aback by Josie's question. "We work together at the university, but her family are local." I don't feel comfortable spilling the beans on Victoria's family tree—it hardly feels like my place. Apparently, I also didn't feel comfortable saying that I'm Victoria's supervisor. So much for letting my hair down and taking my students out for a drink in a relaxed fashion.

Josie arches her eyebrows as if to say, "Yes, and?" But that's all I give her. She only arrived in Upper Chewford last autumn, but working in her mother's pub has put her on a first-name basis with most of the village population. She'll figure it out soon enough.

I pay for the drinks and head back to the table. Victoria looks more relaxed now. When I sit, I'm actually quite pleased with myself for having asked her to meet me here today.

"Thanks for coming." I hold up my glass of wine and she promptly does the same. "Did I hear that right? Did you drive all the way from Oxford?"

Victoria nods. "And I'm driving back later, so only one of these for me."

"Oh." I could have sworn she said she was visiting her family this weekend, but I guess I misunderstood. "I hope it wasn't too much of a bother. If I had known—"

She waves me off, stopping me mid-sentence. "It's a gorgeous drive, even on a day like today."

I nod. "I should know."

"It's quite the commute to do every day," she says.

"I sometimes stay over at the university, but yes, I guess it is. I made the deliberate choice not to live in Oxford when I bought my house here. And, these days, the commute comes in quite handy." I have an opening so quickly already. I watch how Victoria sips from her wine elegantly. I have trouble pulling my gaze away from her mouth. The word luscious springs to mind so easily when I look at her lips.

"For unwinding on the way home?" she asks.

"There's that, but... I've also taken up another habit recently."

She looks at me quizzically and I don't avert my gaze. I need to look at her when I tell her. "That book we were talking about the other day. *Chewed Up in Chewford*."

She nods silently, giving me all the time I need to get to my confession—even though she must have no idea what's coming.

I pull my lips into a small smile before continuing. "I wrote it. I'm H.S. Barr."

Victoria's eyes narrow. "Wait," she says. "You're H.S. Barr." She huffs out a small chuckle. "That's, um, quite a surprise."

"I know it is, Victoria." It's about time I address her with her first name. Especially while telling her this. "Take your time to let it sink in."

"Wow. You have some hidden talents." She's regrouping— perking up under my very eyes, in fact. "Good thing I told you I liked it, then."

"I wouldn't have held it against you if you hadn't. Everyone's entitled to their opinion."

"But I did like it. A lot."

"That's lovely to hear."

Victoria rests her gaze on me. "I googled H.S. Barr extensively and didn't find anything at all connecting them to you, except for the location of the book."

"When I started out, I knew I could only do this if I had complete anonymity. I've only recently started telling people."

"I'm honoured that you would tell me, Prof—"

"Please, call me Helen."

She beams me a wide smile. "So the H.S. stands for Helen Swift."

"And Barr was my mother's maiden name." As I sit talking to Victoria about this, a rush of contentment washes over me. I've held all of this information inside me for so long, while all I ever wanted to do was talk about it. Because writing has become such an essential part of me and to be able to talk freely about it isn't just a relief—it's a source of pure joy.

"What does this have to do with your commute?" Victoria asks.

"I dictate when I drive." I can't help an even wider smile from spreading on my lips.

"Dictate?"

"It's all the rage these days, although it probably makes me look a bit silly, talking to myself in my car like that. But if I didn't write on my commute, I wouldn't know where to find the time." I'm babbling now, but I don't mind.

"I'm so impressed with this." She leans back in her chair, her gaze still on me. "So many people, especially people in the English Department at Oxford, dream of being a writer, and you've just gone and done it."

Every single word Victoria says sounds like music to my ears. There are no questions about the human condition or about how I can possibly combine this with my day job.

"Thank you for saying that, Victoria. I really appreciate it."

Her lips draw into a pout. "Can I ask you something?"

"Shoot." I can hardly refuse her anything now.

"I'm very... happy that you've decided to call me by my first name, but only my mother calls me Victoria, and only when she's annoyed with me or trying to make a point. Everyone else calls me Rory."

"Rory." I let her name roll off my tongue and nod. "Got it. Rory it is from now on."

❧ 22 ❧

RORY

I'm not entirely sure of what's happening in this pub on this rainy Sunday afternoon. For a brief moment, I wonder if I'm being pranked, what with Professor Swift—*Helen*—telling me she's the author of the Chewford novel. It's all a bit surreal.

On top of that, she's going to call me Rory. I've only been here a short while and I've already had so many wins. I might be the one with the silly unrequited crush, but Helen's the one who just confided a secret in me. She wouldn't have done that if she didn't see something—anything—in me.

"On the subject of books," Helen says. "And your research more specifically."

I had completely forgotten this afternoon is supposed to replace our meeting tomorrow. I nod. Even though she's my supervisor, my research is the very last thing I want to talk about this afternoon. I bet if I play my cards right, I can get Helen to reveal a few more things about herself.

"I think the scope would become much too large if you were to include commercial genre fiction." She pushes a strand of wavy blonde hair behind her ear. I'm distracted by the finger with which she performs the action. Oh Christ, this wine seems to have gone straight to my head, which is quite impossible, what with the daily gin diet Jess has got us on.

"I tend to agree." Somewhere in the back of my mind hides what I had prepared on this subject. Professor Swift did ask me to ponder it over the weekend, so I did.

"It would become a completely different dissertation and while there's nothing wrong with changing things now, when you're only just starting, you would have to rethink everything and—"

I can hear her words but I can't seem to absorb them. I am deep in the throes of an impossible infatuation and my brain might be doing something to defend me against it, to restore some balance in my hormone-crazed body.

"Rory?" Helen asks. "Are you listening?"

"Yes, yes," I'm quick to say. "I'm sorry. I'm still processing that I'm sitting across from H.S. Barr." I give her a wide smile, and she stares at me in silence for a few seconds.

"You know what?" She picks up her near-empty wine glass. "Let's talk about this tomorrow instead of on a Sunday afternoon. This is the only time off I've had all week."

"Thanks." I push my glass of wine away from me. "I think the wine is disagreeing with me."

"Shall I get you some water instead?" she asks, concern in her voice. "Or a cup of tea?" She sets her own glass down.

"No. I'm fine. Really."

"I live just down the road. How about we go to my house and I put the kettle on? Settle your stomach before you set off back to Oxford?"

I have great trouble keeping my face in a neutral expression. Is she inviting me into her home? I don't want to jump to any conclusions but it's very hard not to in the state I'm in.

"Yeah, sure. That would be lovely, actually."

"Come on then." She gets up and I follow her home. All the way there, I can't quite believe it.

~

Helen's home is a cottage along the river. It's literally only a few yards away from the pub. Despite the drizzle, the fresh air snaps me out of the daze I lost myself in earlier. I'm happy for the silence, because it allows me to have a stern talk with myself. I really do need to get a grip. And a nice cup of tea. As if a cuppa might have magical healing powers over my state of mind as well as over my body.

Just before we go inside, a woman emerges from the house next door.

"Helen," she starts, and only then seems to spot me. "Oh, sorry, I didn't realise you had company." The woman gives me a thorough once-over.

"Hi Stacey." Helen doesn't introduce me. "I'll talk to you soon." She nods at her neighbour and ushers me inside. I hear them exchange a few more words while I let my gaze roam around the hallway. The decor looks like it's been refurbished recently.

"The perils of living in a tiny village." She smiles at me apologetically. "Everyone's always up in each other's business." She rolls her eyes. "Some more than others, mind you." She leads me to the kitchen, which overlooks a small, very green garden, with nothing but typical Cotswolds rolling hills behind it.

"Nice view," I say.

"Do sit down. How are you feeling?" She fills the electric kettle and flicks it on.

"I'm fine, really." I glance around the kitchen. Obviously, I don't know Helen very well, but her office at the university is always very neatly arranged, and I had expected her kitchen to be the same. It's not.

There are dirty dishes in the sink and a carton of cracked eggs next to the cooker. Around the toaster is a trail of crumbs.

"Excuse the mess. I wasn't expecting guests and, to be honest, cleaning house has been relegated to the bottom of my to-do list for a long time. The cleaning lady's coming tomorrow though, lest you think I live like this all the time." She takes cups and saucers from a cupboard and lays them out. She leans against the kitchen counter while she waits for the kettle to boil.

"Hey, I live in a student flat. I'm really not one to judge." I smile reassuringly. It's as though Helen has become even more relaxed now that we're in her home. Maybe she is. This is her home turf after all. The place where she can be herself.

"You're a student, which is the perfect excuse for a messy home." The kettle whistles and she prepares the tea.

From where I'm sitting, I can see into the lounge and my gaze is drawn to a built-in book case. I can't make out any of the books and I don't imagine she has any H.S. Barr ones on display if she's been keeping her writing identity secret, but a thought pops into my head.

Helen's been the most forward—and I think she has felt the most free—when she's been talking to me about her writing. I'd like to get us back to that vibe for a bit.

"Can I ask you a big favour?"

She nods, eyeing me.

"Do you have any H.S. Barr print copies I could buy?"

"Hm, yes, sure, but—" For once, she's the one who seems flustered around me.

"And could you sign them for me?" I continue.

She brings over our cups of tea and sits at the kitchen table with me. "If you want to, sure, but explain something to me first. Something I've never quite understood." She pauses. "What's the fascination with having an author sign a book?"

"What do you mean?" I'm quite taken aback by her question. Suddenly, I feel like I'm in the middle of an oral exam and a surprise question has been sprung upon me. It's back to me being flustered again.

"I would never ask any author to sign their book for me. It's just a meaningless scribble, really. In fact, I would argue that me signing any of my books devalues it, what with my abysmal signature."

"It's not about what the signature looks like. It's about the sentiment behind it."

"What sentiment?"

At first I thought she was having me on, but Helen seems genuinely interested in my response.

"It's evidence of a heightened connection between the reader and the writer. I think it's human nature to yearn for that." I lift my teacup from its saucer.

"Who's your favourite writer?" she asks.

Put on the spot again. I can hardly say H.S. Barr, even though, sitting in her kitchen over a cup of tea, H.S. Barr is my current favourite person in the whole wide world.

"Hm. John Irving," I blurt out.

"Really?"

"Yes," I confirm.

"That surprises me. I had expected a female writer. Jane Austen or Virginia Woolf or someone like that."

I chuckle. "Because I'm a lesbian?"

She just shrugs. "Anyway, that's another discussion. But let's say John Irving is coming to Oxford and he's doing a book signing. Would you go and ask him to sign one of his books for you?"

"Absolutely. No doubt."

"That is just so strange to me. So... I don't know, forward, I guess."

"Have you ever done a book signing?" I ask.

"Who? Me?" She brings a hand to her chest. "No."

"Ah yes. You're anonymous."

"Regardless of that, I would never go to a book shop and have one of my favourite authors sign a book for me. The whole exchange just seems rather awkward to me."

"Maybe because you've never done it." I sip from my cup of tea. "I have five autographed John Irving novels at home." As I say it, I know it sounds a bit boastful, but I'm really just trying to draw her out. I love it when she engages me in conversation like this. It makes me feel like so much more than her student.

"Lucky you. When did you get those? To my knowledge, John Irving hasn't been to Oxfordshire in the past decade."

"When I was in Toronto a few summers ago."

"Ah, right." She looks at me funnily.

"What?"

She shakes her head. "Nothing."

I decide to let it go. I don't need anything more from this afternoon. I'm already sipping tea with Helen in her kitchen. Jess will be beside herself when I tell her about this. And I'd like to take advantage of this occasion to find out a few other things. I can't just slip the most burning question currently on my mind into this conversation—how are things with Mireille? I need to bide my time and I want to stay in this house a while longer.

"Do you really want me to sign a book for you?" she asks.

"I very much do."

"Why?" Her ice-blue gaze rests on me. Maybe something is beginning to dawn on her. I don't seem to mind so much anymore. "I'm hardly John Irving," she says.

"You're much better looking than John Irving," I blurt out, and immediately the skin of my cheeks feels on fire. Oh shit. I might have overplayed my hand there. "I—I mean, you're my DPhil supervisor. Um, that's why, of course."

She chuckles and stares at me. "Let me get you a few books then," she says drily, and gets up, leaving me alone in the kitchen.

I take the opportunity to get my bearings. I can't seem to help flirting with her. I hear her go up the stairs, followed by some stumbling sounds coming from just above me. Is that her bedroom? I tell myself, once again, to get a grip. But I had never expected to find myself in Helen's house this afternoon. Who knows what other unexpected events might occur?

Two voices war in my head. The one that wants to flirt some more versus the one that represents the cautious side of me. Helen and I have to work together for three more years. I don't want to mess this all up now by doing something very untoward. It's not worth it. The good student in me will always win. Yes, it will.

❦ 23 ❦

HELEN

While I'm still glad I told Victoria about my writing alter ego, I can't help but notice that the afternoon has taken a different turn. I know what flirting looks like and it very much looked like the face of Victoria Carlisle when she told me I was much better looking than John Irving. I'm a couple of decades younger, of course, but I hardly think that's what Rory meant. *Rory.* It feels too intimate to even think of her as merely Rory. It shortens the professional distance between us considerably.

I take my time fetching the books she asked me for—which offers me a chance to examine her motives. Is she genuinely interested in owning some of my novels or was it an easy means of more flirting? Maybe I made a mistake asking her to come to the pub and—what was I even thinking?—into my home. Whatever this is, I have to nip it in the bud straightaway.

I make my way back downstairs and find Victoria in the lounge, examining my bookshelves.

"That's quite the cozy mystery collection," she says, a broad smile painted on those luscious lips of hers. "Any more set in

Chewford?" She looks at my hands which are carrying my own books.

"Not Chewford specifically," I say matter-of-factly, trying to remember my nip-it-in-the-bud plan. The only thing I remember is that I don't have a plan. "But there are plenty set in the Cotswolds, as you can imagine."

Her eyes light up as she focuses more of her attention on me. "Are those for me?"

I nod. "How about I sign them for you later and bring them to tomorrow's meeting?" I'll be damned if I'm going to sign these books in front of her. What would I even write in them? And am I required to scribble down more than my illegible signature? Truth be told, I don't have book-signing etiquette down just yet—and I probably never will.

"Sure. How much do I owe you for them?" She cocks her head. "There's three of them?"

"I can't take your money, Rory." Her nickname seems to roll off my tongue quite easily after all.

"I really must insist on paying."

"You can pay me by stashing these in a secret place. You mentioned a roommate?"

"Jess." She narrows her eyes. "I can do that, of course, but weren't you 'coming out' as H.S. Barr, so to speak?"

"I am, but I want to do it on my own timeline. I don't want it to be a rumour spreading across campus. I don't want whispers behind my back wherever I go." The mere thought of it makes me break out in a shiver.

"You have my word. I won't tell anyone." There's that wide smile again. Rory's face really changes when she smiles, like a light shines down upon her. "Thank you very much, that's very generous of you. I'm chuffed to bits with them. I mean, I will be, once I have them in my hands tomorrow." She sucks her bottom lip into her mouth.

I'm not used to someone saying things like this to me—not

118

in the flesh. I get some fan mail once in a while, but it's not the same as having someone tell me to my face that she enjoyed my books—without questioning me about the human condition.

Alistair also said he enjoyed my book and whilst I do believe him, there was a whiff of best friend's loyalty about that. It's different when Rory tells me she enjoyed my book because I know she read it before she knew I was the one who wrote it.

"Did you really enjoy it?" I could kick myself for asking her, but the urge to know is stronger than myself.

She takes a step closer to me and I don't seem to mind—there are no more nipping-this-in-the-bud thoughts in my head. "I really, *really* did." She pauses. "And what I enjoy even more, Helen..." She looks me straight in the eyes. "Is how you are when you talk about writing and your books and your other career. You seem to come alive when you do and it's so incredibly..." She briefly looks away. "I really shouldn't say what I'm about to say."

"Say it," I ask. "Please." She's standing a few feet away from me, yet she feels so close. She also has me hankering—with a hunger I didn't even know I had in me—for her to continue what she was saying.

Her smile is much less broad. It's peculiar and seductive. "It makes you look very... sexy," she says.

I should take a step back. I should walk away. Disinvite her from my home. A few easy words, that's all it takes. But I haven't been seen like this in a very long time. For someone to tell me that I look sexy when I talk about something that means so much to me is so intoxicating, I never want her to leave my house again. I want to look at her alluring smile for the rest of the afternoon. But I should probably say something now.

"Thank you." *Thank you? Really?*

"You're very welcome, Helen." Rory takes another step closer to me. She's so close now, I can smell her perfume. It's making me feel hazy. "Can I tell you something else?" Her voice has lowered to a whisper.

I swallow hard and nod. I don't want her to stop talking.

She sinks her teeth into her bottom lip again. "What I'm about to say doesn't actually require words."

"In that case..." I can barely push any words past the constriction in my throat. "Won't it be hard—"

She cuts me off by bridging the gap between us and gently pressing her delicious lips to mine. Even though, on some level, I did see this coming, it still takes me by surprise. But what surprises me more is how my body reacts. A flash of heat soars through me, like an animal suddenly roaring awake after a long hibernation.

I respond by slightly opening my mouth and letting her tongue slip between my lips. I'm still holding these damn books, although they're what started this. That's the excuse I make while I'm kissing Rory Carlisle in my living room. She shouldn't have flattered me about my books.

When she brings a hand to my cheek, touching her fingertips to my skin ever so gently, I stop making excuses. I lean into the kiss. A sensation I've missed so much that I'm overcome with the urge to hold her closer. The books drop to the floor, and I don't care how they land or what state they'll end up in. It's unlike me, but so is kissing one of my students.

I cup her jaw in the palms of my hands and pull her closer. This isn't very professorial behaviour. It's really no way to behave at all, but I haven't felt this alive since the moment I pressed the 'publish' button for my first book. That's what this reminds me of. The thrill of possibility blended with a silly sense of pride and tons of insecurity.

Rory's soft tongue dances inside my mouth and I don't want to break the kiss for even the smallest instant out of fear it might stop. When it stops, I'll have to be Professor Swift again.

I'll need to put a stop to it, even though a significant part of me really doesn't want to do that.

Rory catches my bottom lip between her teeth and gently tugs at it. One of her hands is against my neck now, the other in the small of my back, pressing me against her. Even though we're both covered by layers of clothing, I can feel the suppleness and strength of her youth through our clothes. Her breasts push against me and it's their firmness that makes me stop. What am I doing? Have I lost my mind?

I break all contact and, instantly, a huge sense of loss washes over me.

"Rory." All I can do is chuckle half-heartedly. And shake my head.

"Don't expect me to say I'm sorry." She's suddenly very audacious. I can see it glitter in her eyes. Some sort of triumph. Maybe I am some sort of prize to her.

"I think you should leave." I put as much force into my voice as I can.

She looks at me for an instant, her lips pulled into a crooked smile. Those damned lips. If only they weren't so kissable. *Oh, Helen, please. Get a grip.*

"Really?" She keeps looking me in the eye.

I can only nod. I wonder what my face looks like. Does it display the ambivalence I feel?

"I'll see you tomorrow at three," Rory says. "Can't wait." With that, she slips past me, and makes her way out of the lounge.

It's only after I've heard the front door slam shut behind her that I can move again. I sink onto the closest chair I find. I touch a finger to my lips. I can still feel her there. The soft determination she kissed me with. She really came for me with such confidence. She played me. Yes, she did. She knew what my soft spot was and she manoeuvred her way in.

Tomorrow, I will have to truly nip this in the bud.

24

RORY

W hen I'm in my car, I briefly consider driving to my family home because I'm not sure I can make it back to Oxford in the state I'm in. I still can't believe it. I couldn't believe it when she cupped my jaw in her hands. I couldn't believe it when she kissed me back. I went out on a serious limb. Part of me had expected to be booted out of the door immediately with the proviso that I'd need to look for a new supervisor. But Helen kissed me back. She allowed my tongue to slip into her mouth. Granted, she did eventually kick me out, yet I still can't wrap my head around what happened.

Going home in this state is the worse option. My mother would immediately notice I'd been up to something and pepper me with questions. She might annoy me to the point that I just blurt it out, and I can't do that.

The ride to Oxford will give me time to calm down. I start my car and slowly drive past Helen's house. Is she looking out of the window? What is she thinking? Is she wishing she never invited me to Chewford this afternoon?

I go over all the things she told me. It was one intimacy leading to another, really. I promised to keep quiet about H.S.

Barr, which I will do. What I can't promise, not to myself or to Helen, is that I won't tell Jess about that kiss. It will be written all over my face as soon as I step inside the flat. Jess knows me better than anyone. And I need to tell her. But I can't say how it came about. I can't betray Helen's trust.

My mind whirrs like this all the way to Oxford. I'm also very aware that this is the exact route Helen takes every day to go to work. When she drives on this road tomorrow, on the way to her meeting with me, will she be cursing herself or will she be looking forward to seeing me again?

Judging by how abruptly she asked me to leave, I'm banking on the former, all the while feverishly hoping for the latter. I can't wait for three o'clock tomorrow. I can't wait to see her again.

Jess isn't home when I arrive. So much for working on her dissertation every spare minute she can find. I'm glad for the time to compose myself. Out of habit, I head to the drinks cabinet and mix myself a small gin and tonic. I need something to settle my nerves. I don't quite know what to do with myself. I can't get the image of Helen out of my head.

The way she stood there with those books in her hand. I could almost see the war waging in her mind. I could see that if I was ever going to take a chance, it had to be then. I can't even properly explain it to myself. It's what it felt like. This magnetic pull between us. My lips being drawn to hers by an invisible force.

I sit on the chair by the window and watch the sun set over the tiny slice of Oxford I can see. I sip from my drink while wondering how I'm going to deal with this. Because I want more now. I got a taste and I want it all. Something tells me that won't be so easily achieved as asking her to sign a few books for me. I wonder if she will even bring the books tomorrow. I wonder so many things until my phone rings. It's Jess. Thank goodness.

"Are you home?" she asks.

I didn't tell her where I was going this afternoon so I'm spared the third degree. "Yes."

"Take-away?"

"Sure. Pick whatever you like." I won't be able to eat. It seems sacrilege to use my mouth for anything else than kissing Helen Swift. Apart from drinking a gin to steady my nerves.

While I wait for Jess, I go back and forth between telling her or not. If I tell her, she's going to be even more beside herself than I am. I know her. She'll get swept up and spur me on and make me want to do silly things. But I can't keep this to myself either. It's not even an option.

By the time she walks in, I'm bursting to tell her. I've prepared her a drink and we've barely sat when I blurt it out.

"I kissed her." I stare at my food—some sort of vegan lasagne—because for some reason I can't look at Jess.

"Who?" Jess asks. She genuinely has no idea. She doesn't even know where I was this afternoon. I tell her about Helen casually inviting me to The Golden Fleece in Upper Chewford. How I ended up in her house. I leave out the H.S. Barr part, even though it's hard because it's crucial. Jess is too focused on me getting to the kissing to notice any missing parts to my story.

"I can't believe it." She seems to have lost her appetite as well. She leans back and shakes her head. "You're pulling my leg, Rory."

It's misplaced pride I feel, but I feel it nonetheless. And it's lust and hunger—not for vegan lasagne, but for something else entirely. It's the most intoxicating desire. It's most probably also impossible.

"It's true. We kissed."

Jess bangs her hand on the table. "Your lust is no longer unrequited." She tilts her head. "I believe I can actually see it in your face. Is that a hint of I-kissed-the-professor smugness I detect?"

"Stop it, Jess. And she *did* tell me to leave afterwards."

"*After* she came to her senses," Jess says. "Which is a game changer."

"I have my weekly meeting with her tomorrow."

Jess arches her eyebrows and nods. "That should be interesting."

"I'm scared she'll blow me off and ask me to find another supervisor."

"That wouldn't be the worst thing in the world. You wouldn't have a professional relationship any longer, leaving you free to kiss each other as much as you want." She chuckles.

"I don't want another supervisor."

"I'm sure you don't, but what do you want more: Swift as your supervisor or Swift as your lover?"

"Jess, come on."

"Ah... you want both. You always were very ambitious, Rory. It must be that Carlisle blood."

"I don't know what's going to happen."

"But you want to kiss her again?" Jess asks.

"Oh yes."

"Well, then... do it."

"I'm not sure she'll want to kiss me again."

"If she did it once, there's a very good chance she'll want to do it again." Jess pauses. "If you go about it in the right way."

"What's the right way?"

Jess shrugs. "I can't tell you that. Apply your Rory charm. How did you get her to kiss you the first time?"

"I don't want to 'get' her to kiss me. I want her to want to kiss me."

"Christ." Jess shakes her head. "I still can't believe it."

"You can't tell anyone." I forgot to say that right out of the gate. I was a bit too overcome by excitement.

"You don't always have to tell me that, Rory. I know when to keep my mouth shut."

I nod and sip from my drink. I won't be able to sleep, of course. I'll probably end up buying the next H.S. Barr book on my Kindle. I still can't believe that Helen Swift is H.S. Barr. And that she told me that.

❦ 25 ❦

HELEN

All throughout Monday morning, I find myself checking my watch. I simultaneously dread and look forward to facing Rory. I've prepared a little speech, but I'm not sure I'll be able to actually utter the words when I need to. She seems to have a strange power over me.

Of course, I know that I have to tell her that what happened was a mistake. I've even managed to explain it to myself in a way that satisfied me. I opened up to her. I made myself the most vulnerable I've been since I started writing fiction. And her reaction to it was perfect. So perfect that I confused it with something else. Something my life has been lacking for a while. I'm not going to tell her all that in detail. I'll give her the shortest version possible. I'm her supervisor. I'll keep it professional.

I'm glad that I haven't bumped into Sarah or Alistair. Sarah did text me last night to invite me to dinner with her and Joan next weekend.

I try to focus on my tasks at hand. I have to approve dissertation topics for the third years. But every few minutes, an image of Rory's lips seems to pop up in my brain. It's distracting. For that reason alone, I need to put a stop to whatever this thing is between us this afternoon.

This morning, when I should have been dictating my next novel on the way to work, I found myself rehearsing my little speech instead. I actually have it recorded in case I need reminding what it is I need to tell Rory.

It was easy enough in the car. I fear it might be a touch more difficult when Rory's sitting across from me.

I eat a quick sandwich in the privacy of my office, watching the clock tick by. I'm the superior in this hierarchy. I'm the older one. The wiser one. It's my responsibility to tell her that it was all a misunderstanding and that, most certainly, nothing can ever come of it.

I've noticed students having a mild crush on me before. It comes with the territory of teaching. But I've never had to deal with it in this way. I've never kissed a student before, even though Rory's not technically my student. It very much feels like she is. Now I can't wait for it to be three o'clock. Or even better, a quarter past. Then all of this will be over and I can get on with my life again. Forget about this frankly embarrassing episode. I have plenty to do to distract myself.

I glance at the stack of three books I brought, regardless of my decision to not give them to Rory after all. It sums up all the current contradictions racing through me. Things would have been so much easier if Mireille hadn't met someone else—if I'd made my move quicker. I might have been going out with a woman of a perfectly respectable age right about now, instead of pining for a girl in her twenties.

I haven't signed the books. It seemed like a preposterous thing to do after what happened. Like a sort of validation of me responding to her kiss. Besides, she shouldn't have kissed me in the first place.

My mind keeps racing like this as time passes. Until it's three o'clock and Rory knocks on my door.

~

"Hi." Rory barges in with a big smile. I ignore it. I keep my face in the most neutral expression I can muster.

"Please, sit." I make sure my voice doesn't convey any of the weaknesses I've been beset with since yesterday afternoon—because that's exactly what they are, weaknesses.

"How are you?" she asks.

The question takes me aback. It's the way in which she asks it. She's more confident than usual.

"I'm fine, but... I need to make some things crystal clear." I find it hard to look at her. How much clearer do I have to make myself after kicking her out of my house yesterday?

"Are those my books?" she asks, looking away from me.

When I arrived this morning, the first thing I did was take those three books from my bag and put them on my desk. Another first. It felt exhilarating to put them on the desk—the desk that belongs to my other life.

"I'm surprised you have them on display like that." Rory looks at me again. Her smile is different. Warm and encouraging. This is the version of her I find hardest to resist, but it also reminds me why that kiss happened.

"I haven't signed them," I blurt out. Way to go, Helen. "Look, Rory, what happened yesterday, for me, was a direct result of you being so... lovely and encouraging about my books and my writing. I confused it with something else. I'm sorry for what happened. It really shouldn't have. I hope you can understand that."

She nods slowly while sinking her teeth into her bottom lip. I really wish she wouldn't do that.

"I completely understand your doubts," she says. "I even understand what you're saying. It makes sense in a way, but..." She pins her gaze on me. "That's not how it is for me."

"Whatever it is you think you feel for me, you're going to have to get past it."

"I don't want to lose you as my supervisor, Helen." She shrinks a little, but not too much. It still very much feels like Rory's the one in control here.

I wave off her comment. "You won't. I'm very interested in your research and I want to be a part of that. But that's it. That's where I have to draw the line. I need you to tell me that you're hearing this."

"Sure." She may agree with me with her words, but her eyes tell a different story. They sparkle while she draws her lips into an irresistible smile again. "But tell me this, Helen..." She pauses and I hardly recognise her in that moment. She hasn't come to merely flirt. She has come to seduce me. I have to be strong. It's the only way. Pretend I have no feelings for her. "Honestly... are you sure you don't want to kiss me again?"

She has me opening and closing my mouth, like a fish on dry land. She's starting to make me feel ridiculous.

"Quite sure," I reply. "Now shall we talk about your research?"

"Yes." She sits up a little straighter. "But just so there's no doubt about it: I really enjoyed kissing you. I feel zero ambivalence about it. I think you are an amazing woman. You're smart and gorgeous and a damn good kisser." The smile has faded from her lips.

"Rory. Please." I need to find a way to steel myself. Or maybe I do need to consider recusing myself as her supervisor. For my own sake—as well as hers, of course. "It was just a kiss and it was a mistake, no matter which way you look at it. So let's move on." I take a deep breath.

She nods. When I glance at her briefly, I don't see the sparkle in her eyes anymore.

"I've thought about what you said about my research

yesterday in the pub." Her voice has the lightest tremble to it. So subtle, I shouldn't even be noticing it. But I do.

"We don't have to do this today, Rory." I curse myself for feeling sorry for her—or maybe it's not just her I'm feeling sorry for. "How about we pick this back up next week. Give ourselves some time to deal with this." My turn to throw in an encouraging smile. That's what I'm here for, after all. "I take it you have plenty to do until then."

"Yeah." She doesn't get up. I can see how torn she is. It all plays out on her face. It suddenly hits me that this must be much harder for her than it is for me. My first instinct is to walk over to her and hug her. To tell her everything will be all right. But that would be a grave mistake.

"I'm so sorry this happened." I'm sorry I didn't exhibit more self-control, I think. "I don't want to be unkind, but we have to be realistic."

"I know. It's fine." She tries a smile but it falls flat. "Really. I'll see you next week." She gets up. "It was a mistake." She walks to the door. Before exiting, she turns to me, and says, "I read the next book in your series last night. I really enjoyed it."

Before I have a chance to thank her, she's out of the door. I sit staring at it for a good long while, before I can move another muscle.

This girl has gotten under my skin. I have let her. I glance at the stack of books. Maybe I need to write it off me. Give my main character a romance plot with a younger woman to lose herself in—all the while solving murders in the Cotswolds, of course.

❦ 26 ❧

RORY

As soon as I leave Helen's office, I decide to drown my sorrows in The Maiden's Head. It's not as if my supervisor has given me any other tasks. She basically told me to get over it. So I will.

It's early in the afternoon and the pub is near empty, which suits me just fine. I find a seat at the corner of the bar and order a gin and tonic.

"We have a new gin in," the bartender informs me. "Yolanda, from a small distillery in the Cotswolds. He shows me the bottle. "Do you want to try it?"

"Sure, as long as you make it a double."

"Coming right up."

I take my Kindle from my bag. I've already bought and downloaded the third H.S. Barr book that's currently available. I wasn't lying when I told Helen that I enjoyed her books. I really like the way she writes and the main character of her series—Detective Inspector Orla Parish—is quite swoon-worthy. But I'm biased, of course. But no, I'm not. I liked the book Alistair recommended even before I knew that H.S. Barr was Helen Swift.

Helen Swift who is claiming confusion for kissing me back.

I take a large sip from my drink. I wish Jess was here but she teaches back-to-back tutorials on Monday afternoon. A group of mostly male students walks into the pub. I watch them as they find a table near the window. One of them heads to the bar to order and gives me a good once-over. I give him the death stare—the opposite, I think, of the look I tried to give Helen earlier in her office. He looks away, just like Helen did.

I start reading the book while drinking steadily and wallowing in self-pity.

"Must be one hell of a book." The voice comes from just next to me. I wasn't even reading. I was day-dreaming while keeping my eyes trained on my Kindle so that no one would notice.

"Professor Fleming." It's nice to see a friendly face.

He tilts his head. "Alistair, I beg you."

I give him a nod accompanied by a smile.

"What are you having?" he asks.

"Oh, really, you don't have to—"

"Rory," he says with the most authority I've heard him speak. "It only takes one glance at you to see you could really do with another."

I don't have the wherewithal to argue with him. "I'll have the same again, please. Gin and tonic."

"Do you mind if I join you or do you prefer to sulk in private?" He beams me a big smile. He has the kindest brown eyes. I never noticed before. He's also one of Helen's best friends, so of course I want him to join me. It would also be very rude to have him buy me a drink and then ask him to leave me in peace.

"Please." I gesture at the barstool next to mine.

"The look on your face tells me I shouldn't ask whether you want to talk about it. But if I'm wrong, well, fire away. I'm not a bad listener."

I just shake my head.

Our drinks are delivered pronto—despite the noise the table of students are making, it's still not very busy in the pub—and we tip our glasses to each other.

Alistair doesn't seem to take offence at my muteness. "I will, however, ask you what you thought of that book I sent you."

I have to chuckle. I briefly wonder what would have happened if he hadn't recommended *Chewed Up in Chewford* to me. Would I have found myself in Helen's lounge, so compelled to kiss her I couldn't stop myself?

I show him the open page on my Kindle. "Reading the third in the series right now, actually."

"And that for a DPhil in English Lit. Would you call it a guilty pleasure?"

I ignore his question because I have a very pressing one of my own. "Why did you recommend that particular book to me?" I examine his face closely.

He doesn't bat an eyelid. "Because you told me your family live in Chewford and the book's called *Chewed Up in Chewford*."

"And you like reading books set in Chewford?" I understand why he's being coy with me, but surely he must know.

"I very much do. I've been to those parts a few times myself. Your supervisor lives there and she's one of my best friends."

I don't have the energy to keep up the pretence. And knowing what I know about Helen, she must have given him an earful after I told her that Alistair recommended her book to me.

"I know Professor Swift is H.S. Barr."

His eyes grow wide. "You're very clever then. How did you find out?"

"She told me." A small burst of pride courses through me.

"She told you?" He takes a sip. "Wow. She's really opening up about it then."

"The main character is a lesbian, so I asked if self-published books should be included in my research. That's when she confided in me that she's the one who wrote the book." And not long after, I kissed her, I want to scream.

Alistair nods. "I understand why she kept it hidden for so long, but I'm glad Helen's telling more and more people now."

"They're really good books. She should be proud of them."

"Exactly." He takes another large sip from his drink. "So, now will you tell me why you're drinking during the day?"

"I'm a student. That's what we do."

"Maybe some of them do." He glances at the boisterous table by the window. "But I didn't have you pegged as one of those."

"I could ask the same of you and you don't have the excuse of being a student." I can't tell him the truth so I need to diffuse his focus.

"I'm surrounded by students, which is enough reason to come in here and have a tipple in the middle of the afternoon."

"So you can be surrounded by even more of us?" This new gin is very tasty, so I take a long drag from my straw.

Alistair chuckles, but his chuckle fades quickly. "Will the sudden death of a family member do?" He picks up his glass and drains it in one go. "A third cousin, but still, he was way too young to die. I've come to face my own mortality at the bottom of this glass, I guess."

"I'm so sorry." A teacher crush does seem extremely silly in the face of death.

"We're all going to die at some point, Rory. We might as well make the best of the time we have." He regards me intently. "Sometimes, that entails hiding in a dark corner of the pub." He gestures the bartender over. "So, have one more with me, will you?"

"Of course." I'm feeling the effects of the gin, but I'm happy to have another—and to have Alistair's company.

"What's your excuse for moping?" he asks after having placed the order.

"Earlier you said you weren't going to ask me."

"That's true. I did say that. But I never said I was a man of my word, did I?" He grins.

"Maybe I'll tell you after I've finished this." I pick up my fresh gin and tonic.

"Not maybe, Rory. I'll make sure that you do."

~

"Can you repeat that, please?" Alistair says.

"I kissed Helen and she kissed me back." We're on our fourth gin and both far from sober at this point. We've moved from the bar to a nook in the back room of the pub.

"No way." He shakes his head vehemently. "That's simply not possible. I've known Helen Swift for a very long time and she would never do such a thing."

"She claims that she confused elation about my reaction to her H.S. Barr confession with the desire to kiss me back." I'm so glad to be able to talk about it. And this is the only way. Drunk, in a dark corner of the pub.

"Is today April Fool's Day?" Alistair asks. "Did they change the date? Are we having a second one in October?"

"It's okay if you don't believe me. In fact, the more incredulous you are about it, the more helpful it is to me." I'm not even sure of what I'm saying anymore. It's more drunken babble than anything else.

"Wait. I believe *you*." He glances at me. His eyes are glazed over. "It's more that I can't believe Helen. It's so unlike her."

"That may be so... but it really wasn't that hard to get her to kiss me." I revel in the memory for a few seconds.

"And now she doesn't want to kiss you anymore." He juts out his bottom lip, as if in deep contemplation.

"I'm glad she still wants to be my supervisor."

He briefly lifts a few fingers. "You're consenting adults. These things happen. It's just the way of the world. I should know."

"Has it happened to you?" The booze is making me very forward.

"I'm the rare gay who doesn't fancy younger men." He bursts out laughing. "But, my partner Jack used to be a professor."

What he says doesn't really register. I can only think of Helen. "Do you think Helen will come around? That there's even the slightest chance?" I might as well ask him now. It's a unique opportunity.

He huffs out a slow breath. "Honestly, I don't think there's much chance. Then again, fifteen minutes ago, I would never have believed Helen would go around kissing students, so there's that... People can—and always will—genuinely surprise you."

"You can't tell her that I told you, Alistair. You have to promise me that you won't."

"No." He shakes his head. "That's not a promise I can keep. For all my many virtues, keeping this a secret will not be one of them. Helen's my friend. She's probably agonising over this like crazy. I have to be there for her."

"Please tell me you're the one pulling my leg now." Panic streaks through me. "She might drop me as her DPhil student if she finds out I told you."

"Look, don't worry about it. I'll make it so she's the one who tells me. I'm pretty good at that." He winks at me. "In that respect, your secret's *fairly* safe with me."

I let my head fall into my hands. "Shit. I shouldn't have told you."

"Rory." He puts his hand on my shoulder. "You told me for a

reason. It's for the greater good. And you know... I have some sway over Helen." He lifts my head out of my hands. "If you know what I mean."

All I know is that Alistair is very drunk—as am I—and I might have blown things even more.

27

HELEN

I don't much feel like a drive back and forth to Oxford on a Saturday evening, but that's how it is when you live in the middle of nowhere and your closest friends don't.

Alistair called me earlier this week from his hometown where he was attending a funeral, asking me to meet him and Jack for a drink before we all head to dinner at Sarah's.

I happily said yes for various reasons. The first one being that he sounded so glum when I spoke to him, I would have said anything to make him feel better. I also prefer not to arrive at Sarah's alone. Not when I'm meeting her new partner.

The third reason is that I'm seriously considering telling him and Jack about Rory. If anyone can understand my predicament, it's the two of them.

I have to face her again on Monday and I haven't been able to get her out of my head. I've scolded myself. I tried breathing exercises every time she popped into my thoughts, but I was beginning to get out of breath because of the sheer number of times I forced myself to inhale and exhale deeply. I even considered asking Stacey if she had any other new acquaintances she could set me up with. That's how bad I seem to have it. It's unseemly and undignified, but there it is.

What I see projected on the back of my eyelids as soon as I close my eyes rotates between two distinct images. One is her face, just before she kissed me. Her lips inviting, her eyes glittering. The other one is the disillusion in her eyes when I asked her to leave my office last Monday, when I dismissed her. How the light in her dimmed. That's the one I have most trouble shaking off.

We meet in a wine bar where few students go. I haven't seen Jack in a long time. They both hug me as if I've come back from the dead.

"What a warm welcome," I say as I sit down.

"Wait until you taste this." Alistair shows me the bottle of wine they've ordered. "And yes, you're drinking tonight, darling. We made up the guest room for you."

"We'll see about that." Alistair says the exact same thing every time I meet him in Oxford in the evening. Sometimes I take him up on his offer, sometimes I don't. Tonight, it will really all depend on what the topic of conversation turns out to be. I guess it might also depend on Sarah and Joan. I can't predict what effect seeing my ex with her new partner will have on me. To see new love in action. Will it make me pine for Rory even more?

Alistair tells me about the funeral he attended. As usual, he's the one who talks a mile a minute while Jack listens and sends me frequent warm smiles. I've known them for such a long time, I've long forgotten about the age difference between them. And how their affair started.

"What's been going on with you, Helen?" Jack asks once Alistair stops to take a breather.

"Did you tell him?" I ask Alistair.

"About your extracurricular writing activities?" Alistair nods. "He's my better half. Of course, I've told him. Was I not allowed to?"

I always expected Alistair to tell Jack and I never expressly asked him not to.

"I'm so happy for you, Helen. I really am." Jack is such a gentleman. "If not a tad offended that you didn't tell us sooner."

"I needed time." I look into Jack's kind face.

"You almost made me want to read fiction. *Almost*."

Alistair rolls his eyes. "Sometimes I wonder how I can be married to someone who doesn't read novels."

The wine is excellent and we soon order a second bottle. Sarah lives a five-minute walk away. And I have something to tell them. Except I have no idea how.

"Alistair's been going through a bit of an existential crisis this week," Jack says. "With his cousin dying."

"He was forty-five years old." Alistair's voice sounds a little wine-soaked. "Can you imagine that? I'm forty-three. He was only two years older than me. One minute he was going about his life, and the next, he dropped dead."

"He's been coping really well with it," Jack says. "He came home completely plastered last Monday."

"I went to the pub for one drink, just to digest the news, but I ran into someone I knew and you know how these things can go sometimes," Alistair days.

"Someone I'd never heard of." Jack grins at me. "It was a woman, though, so I'm not too worried."

Alistair fixes his gaze on me. "I went on a bender with Rory Carlisle."

The mention of Rory's name makes my muscles tense up. "Rory?" is all I can say.

"The one and only." He keeps his gaze on me for a fraction too long. Surely Rory wouldn't have told him anything. I need to find out.

"Why was she on a bender?" I try to keep my voice even.

"Oh, you know what young people are like. This and that, I

guess. She'd just had a bad day, I think." Alistair quickly drinks from his wine.

I get the impression he's not telling me the full story.

"I told Rory I'm H.S. Barr. Since you were so kind to recommend *Chewed Up in Chewford* to her." I look him straight in the eye.

"If I had known she had such a crush on you, Helen, I might have refrained. To not stoke the fires and such." He looks me right back in the eye.

"Am I missing something here?" Jack asks.

"Helen's doctorate student has a massive crush on her," Alistair is quick to say. "And who can blame her, really?" He all but bats his lashes.

"What did Rory tell you?"

"She's a fan of H.S. Barr *and* of Helen Swift," Alistair says. "That about sums it up." His lips form into a mischievous smile. "She was reading one of your books when I ran into her at the pub."

This is my chance to tell them. What else am I going to do to quench the turmoil in my gut? Finish this bottle of wine on my own and embarrass myself in front of Sarah's new girlfriend?

I lean over the table. "I think I know why Rory was so upset."

They both slant their faces towards me.

"She came to my house last Sunday. We... um..." Turns out I have no idea how to tell them this. But this is Alistair and Jack. If they don't get it, no one ever will. "We kissed." There. It's out. I don't immediately feel better though.

"You kissed your student?" Jack looks at me incredulously.

"She kissed me, to be exact."

"But you didn't push her away?" Jack asks.

I shake my head.

"Oh, Helen." Jack looks at Alistair. "She's doing a Jack and Alistair, honey. Isn't it wonderful?"

Alistair just sniggers.

"I'm doing no such thing. I asked her to leave and told her in no uncertain terms that it was all a big misunderstanding. A mistake, even."

Jack shrugs. "Very much along the line of expectations." He lowers his voice. "And now you can't get her out of your head?"

"Look at us, Helen," Alistair says before I can respond—for which I'm glad. "You're basically reliving our origin story."

"No, no, no." As much as I adore them, and respect their relationship, that's not something I want for myself. But I can't really tell them that.

"You can try to fight it..." Jack adds.

"It was just a kiss. And on Monday when we had our weekly meeting, I repeated my stance on the matter. That's probably why she was upset when you ran into her. She's had a good bender so I'm sure she's over it by now."

"This isn't about Rory," Alistair says. "Right now, it's about you."

"I think we should get going. We don't want to keep Sarah and Joan waiting." I push my empty glass away from me.

"Helen." Jack's tone is firm and earnest. "Don't let a good thing pass you by because of... possible embarrassment or anything of the sort. Alistair is the best thing that ever happened to me and I'm not just saying that because he's sitting next to me."

I shake my head. "It's not like that."

"I think the lady doth protest too much," Alistair says.

"You can talk to us any time you need." Jack puts a hand on my arm. "About anything you want to. Okay?"

"Yes, sure, but..." I've run out of things to say. I thought telling someone would give me clarity, but it seems to only have confused me more. "Can we keep this between us?" I make to get up. "I don't want Sarah to know."

"Of course." They both nod. "Now let's go meet the plumber," Alistair says.

~

"So let me get this right," Joan says, looking at Jack and Alistair. "You taught Economics and he was a student at your university, but not in one of your classes."

Alistair sits there nodding as though he's actually proud of how he and Jack got together. He probably is. He's the kid that got the teacher.

"How did you meet?" Joan continues to pepper them with questions. She's not what I had expected at all. She's extremely direct and there's absolutely nothing posh about her. I just never thought Sarah would be interested in someone like that, but as it turns out, she's quite besotted with Joan—who's come to this dinner with a pair of Oxford professors dressed in jeans and a simple t-shirt. It looks clean enough, I guess, but it also looks as though she's worn it on a lot of jobs. Earlier, when she lifted her arm to curl it around Sarah, I spotted a hole in its threadbare armpit.

"The old-fashioned way," Jack says. "We noticed each other on campus and around town."

"And this was allowed?" she asks.

When I glance at Alistair, I can't help but wonder if he and Jack ended up talking about this for my benefit. To remind me that I have options. But Rory is not an option for me.

"It was most certainly frowned upon," Jack says. "It did ruin my reputation at the University of Gloucestershire, so I ended up resigning. But you know what? I was all the happier for it in the end."

"So was I, because he became a money-maker instead of a stuffy Economics professor."

"May I remind you that you are now a stuffy English Literature professor," Jack says.

"There's nothing stuffy about the English Department, darling. Look at the two babes who work there with me."

"This one sure is," Joan says, and smiles at Sarah, who sits there basking in Joan's glow.

How did I end up in the middle of this couples' love fest? At least Sarah used to be single. She had so many hang-ups, I was always sure I'd beat her to a new relationship. Clearly, I was wrong.

"How about you, Helen?" Joan aims her dark gaze at me. "You must have some hot ladies sniffing around." She gives a loud cackle of a laugh.

I see Sarah tense up at this remark. Maybe she's jealous. Ha, that would be the day. Alistair clears his throat, but there's no way I'm bringing up my kiss with Rory in front of Sarah and her new girlfriend.

"I haven't really had time for a relationship since Sarah and I broke up."

"Oh yeah, that's right. I'm reading one of your books right now. It's really great."

Joan sure knows how to endear herself to me. "Thank you."

"You must always make time for love, though." She would say that, what with being newly smitten.

"I'm very happy on my own," I hear myself say, which isn't always true.

"Good for you." Joan cocks her head. "But does that mean you're available? I might know someone..." She waggles her eyebrows.

Sarah must notice my discomfort, because she gets up and asks me if I'd like to help her with something in the kitchen.

"I'm quite available," I say, before I join Sarah.

"What do you think?" Sarah asks when we're both in the kitchen.

"Joan's lovely." I give her a smile.

"I can hear you talking about me," Joan shouts from the living room.

We both burst out laughing.

"She's quite something," I whisper.

Sarah nods enthusiastically. "I know." I can hardly believe it when she actually grabs my arm. "I'm so happy, Helen. She makes me so happy."

"I'm glad."

"I know things didn't work out with Mireille, but don't deny yourself this feeling," Sarah urges. "For any reason."

"Didn't you need help with something?" While I can appreciate Sarah's sentiment, I don't need to take lessons in love from my ex.

"Oh yes, can you open another bottle of wine, please?" She smiles at me in a way that I don't really know how to deal with. For a brief moment, I wonder if she's seen through me. That she knows about my stolen kiss with Rory. Then I shake it off. Sarah doesn't have any psychic powers and I know any residual feelings I might still have for Rory will dissolve quickly enough.

As I bring the wine to the dining room, I consider Alistair's offer of staying the night at their house. I might very well take him up on it.

✣ 28 ✣

RORY

When I wake on Sunday, I briefly consider another impromptu excursion to Upper Chewford. But this time, I don't have an invitation to meet Professor Swift at the pub—I only have instructions to forget about her and that kiss as quickly as possible. Besides, I'm supposed to have brunch with Jess and a few friends at one of those places that offer free-flow mimosas. It seems like a good idea if I'm going to try and forget all about Helen.

I've had plenty of time to recover from Tuesday's hangover, although I do wonder how Alistair fared. I haven't seen him at the university all week, although that's not entirely uncommon. It also reminds me of what he said. *I have some sway with Helen.* Does he really? And if he did, what would it mean?

I shrug off the thought and get out of bed. As I do, my Kindle falls to the floor. I fell asleep while reading last night. I finished the last available H.S. Barr book. Maybe it's for the better that there's no more available.

When I walk into the hallway, I notice Jess's bedroom door is open. I peek inside and see her bed hasn't been slept in. Someone got lucky. I check my phone. No messages. She must have gotten really lucky then. I suppose she'll tell me all about it at brunch.

~

The guy Jess has brought along is so incredibly full of himself, I gorge myself on mimosas much more than I otherwise would—just to drown out the sound of his annoying voice.

To my disgust, Jess says, "Rory's a Carlisle, you know." Does she actually like this guy?

I excuse myself because I don't want to have this conversation. As I make my way to the ladies' room, still rolling my eyes, I notice a group of three entering the restaurant. My stomach drops all the way to the floor. Our eyes meet and I find myself looking straight into Helen's face. She's flanked by Alistair and an older man.

My first thought is: what is she doing in Oxford on a Sunday? But it's none of my business and I really don't know that much about Helen's life. Then I consider perhaps moving my body and actually making my way to the loo.

"Rory," Alistair shouts. "How's your hangover?" He smiles at me, then says to the man he's with, "She's the one who got me drunk last Monday."

I walk over to them—it would be very impolite not to say hello—only to find myself awkwardly following them as they're being seated.

"Lovely to meet you," the man Alistair's with says while holding out his hand. "And I won't hold it against you, Rory."

Helen hasn't said anything yet. I hardly dare to look in her direction.

"I don't suppose you can join us?" Alistair asks.

Helen clears her throat now and even though it's a dismissive sound she's making, my gaze is drawn to her.

She looks a little tired, but nothing can take away from her appeal. I'm instantly overcome with that tug inside of me again. With that desire to press my lips to hers.

"I'm here with friends." My voice sounds all funny.

"Of course you are." Alistair brings a hand to my arm. "Maybe a coffee later?"

"Sure." He's left the door wide open for me and I'm not sure if I should be grateful to him for that or not. "That would be nice."

Helen gives me the slightest of nods. If Alistair has exercised his *sway* with her, it's not showing at all.

"Please excuse me." I finally head to the toilets, where I sit behind the locked door of the cubicle long enough to catch my breath and recover from coming face to face with Helen. If Jess sees her, it's going to be hard to control her. Luckily she's focussed on that twat of a guy.

While I wash my hands, I look at my reflection in the mirror. I practice my smile for when I walk out and pass Helen's table. I shake my head at myself. It might be a little harder to get over this than I had expected.

Then the door opens and in walks Helen. All thoughts leave my brain for an instant and an involuntary smile spreads on my lips. Then my mind starts racing. This can't be a coincidence. She saw me come in here. She must have something to say to me.

"Please don't join us for coffee later," she whispers.

My heart sinks. Hope still surges through me when I see her. I can't help myself. But maybe if she squashes it enough times, it will disappear after a while.

"Okay."

"Alistair knows," she says.

Oh shit. I hope he didn't tell her I was the one to spill the beans.

"So it would be very uncomfortable for me if you joined us," she continues.

I nod while, inwardly, sighing with relief. "Got it."

"But, Rory..." Someone else walks into the ladies' toilets and the space is suddenly very cramped. Damn it. Thank goodness it isn't Jess.

"Can I see you later? Today, I mean."

"Of course." I have to keep myself from nodding too eagerly.

"Somewhere private?" she asks.

I nod. "Come to my place. I'll make sure my roommate isn't home." That shouldn't be a problem, what with Jess's current infatuation with Mister Twat. "I'll text you the address." My heart goes from sinking to leaping all the way into my throat.

Helen disappears into a cubicle without saying anything else. My only challenge now is keeping a straight face while I join Jess and the others.

❧ 29 ❧

HELEN

I'm not sure why I'm doing this. Maybe it was seeing Sarah so smitten with Joan last night. Or maybe it's what Alistair and Jack said when we were having drinks. Or maybe, it's very simply the fact that when I'm faced with Rory I can't stop myself. I suppose it's a little bit of everything.

My finger trembles when I ring the bell. I feel caught out already just standing in front of this building. But I need to relax. I'm not entirely sure why I'm here yet, but I should trust my instincts. Or is that the exact thing that will get me into the most trouble?

I'm buzzed in and make my way to the first floor. Rory's flat is in a beautiful Victorian house. I seem to remember that a lot of property in Oxford is owned by the Carlisles.

The door is ajar when I arrive. Rory quickly closes it behind me.

I glance around. I would have expected the home of two DPhil students to be a lot messier than this. I'm still embarrassed about the state of my own house when I invited Rory in. It was only a week ago, yet it feels like I've lived a lifetime since.

"Lovely place." I walk to the window. Maybe if I fix my gaze on something other than Rory, I will feel more at ease.

"Thanks. Can I get you anything?" Rory seems a bit jumpy. "A cup of tea?"

I nod. "That would be lovely."

While she disappears into the kitchen, I wonder, again, what I'm doing here. When we ran into her at the restaurant, the first thought that popped into my head was that I wanted to see her again. As soon as possible. But I'm usually not one to give in to impulses like that. Yet here I am. It's like I was pulled towards this place. As though I had very little to do with my own actions at all. But, of course, I have everything to do with them. I was the one who suggested we talk. I was the one who walked here. I had many occasions to stop myself from coming here, yet I didn't take any of them. Because I didn't want to. Because I want something else.

I go into the kitchen where I hear Rory rummaging around.

"Hey." Her smile is as broad and bright as ever. "Tea should be ready in a few."

She can't really think I walked into the kitchen to inquire about the tea. Can she tell when she looks at me? How much I want her? How much of myself—and my common sense—I'm ignoring while I stand here in her kitchen. I could plead some sort of romantic insanity, but this isn't romance and I'm much too sane for that.

It's lust. I want her. I want to feel her lips on mine again. I want to feel her yield under my touch. I want to feel that sharp, sudden rush of aliveness I experienced last Sunday.

"Helen?" she asks. The kettle starts boiling and it pulls me from my thoughts. "Are you all right?"

She switches off the kettle and I take a step towards her.

"Forget about the tea." I reach for her wrist.

Forget about everything, I say to myself, silently.

"Rory." I look into her eyes. It feels silly to say anything more. What else could I say, anyway? She's not pulling away. I trace my fingers from her wrist, over her arm, all the way to her cheek. I have a moment of clarity. A moment in which I'm convinced there's nothing wrong with what I'm about to do. So, I lean in and kiss her.

All week, while I was trying to persuade myself this was not what I wanted, I knew it was exactly what I wanted. And how could it possibly be wrong when it feels this good? The instant our lips meet, Rory pulls me close, as though I am her long-lost lover. As though she is nothing less than ecstatic to welcome my lips back on hers.

She brings her hands to the back of my neck and pulls me closer. We've barely even spoken. This is how we communicate in this moment—and I hope for the rest of the afternoon. Because I can't ask her to leave today. I can leave of my own volition, but that's the last thing I want to do. I want to kiss her forever.

Kissing Rory is a completely unique experience—or maybe I've forgotten what it feels like to kiss a woman. No. I could never forget. But ever since she came to my office for the first time, it's her mouth, her luscious lips, I've been drawn to. It must have started then. The seed of this desire must have been planted then.

"Oh, Helen," she says, when we break from our kiss for a short moment. She looks me in the eye and I lose myself in her dark, fiery gaze. She presses me against the kitchen counter and the contours of her body nestling against mine make me lose myself further in the kiss.

My hands wander into her hair and it feels so intimate because it adds to the kiss, to the passionate dance of our tongues, and then I know for certain that I won't be leaving Rory's flat any time soon.

She's the one who pulls away first. Her lips are swollen, making them look even more kissable. She looks at me while taking a few deep breaths.

"I have to say..." She pauses. "I wasn't expecting that."

"Neither was I." It sounds so silly. Anything I will say now will sound like the silliest thing I've ever said.

"I'm a bit confused," she says. "Last time we spoke, you told me in no uncertain terms to forget about that kiss, yet here we are. Kissing again."

"Don't give me the third degree now, Rory. I'm just..." I don't know what to say next. I don't want to talk.

"Looks to me as if you just want to kiss me." She tugs at my hand.

I nod while sucking my bottom lip into my mouth. I can still taste her on my lips.

"How about we kiss in a room other than the kitchen?" she asks.

"I don't care *where* we kiss." I pull her close to me. Our lips are a mere inch away from each other. "As long as we kiss."

I don't lean in and neither does she. She gazes into my eyes. "What happened?" she asks.

"Nothing." I slant forward, but she pulls away a little. It only makes me want to kiss her more.

"Doesn't look like nothing to me." Her voice is a mere whisper.

"Rory," I groan, and I notice how saying her name has a hypnotising effect on me. "Don't you get it?"

Her lips draw into a small smile.

"I want you," I say, and it sets me free. I don't allow her to pull away again. Our lips meet again and again and her hands are in my hair now as well. Her breasts push against mine. Her thigh slides between my legs.

This isn't just a kiss anymore. I have a decision to make.

Even though there's nothing rational about this. My body is nothing more than a well of emotion and lust and I know I can't reason myself out of this. I'm too far gone. Rory's body on mine feels too good, too right. Too much like something I've wanted for a very long time.

30

RORY

Helen kisses me again and a voice inside my head keeps repeating that this isn't possible. That I must be dreaming. That this isn't really happening.

But maybe I saw it in her glance at the restaurant. I saw something. Alistair is right—he does seem to have the utmost sway over her. What on earth did he say?

It doesn't matter. We're kissing again. No, we're doing much more than kissing. This is a far cry from that first kiss we shared last week. Every time we touch, I feel Helen's desire for me. It's palpable. It's all around us. Her fingers claw for me, her mouth yearns for me. If we keep going like this, there's only one way this will end. In my bed. The thought is almost too much to bear. It makes me shiver. It makes me claw right back for her.

I've dreamed of this moment. Not often, because I didn't allow my mind to go fully there, but I can't always control my thoughts. Fragments like this have shown up in my head, but even in my imagination, Helen was never like this. She seems to want me to an extent I never deemed possible. And for a brief moment, I wonder if I have to protect myself. If she's going to blow cold again after blowing so very hot today. If next week she's going to ask me to forget about it all again.

But right now, I'm in the middle of our own private, scorching hot Sunday afternoon. If, tomorrow, she asks me to forget about it for the rest of my life, I will always have this afternoon. I will always have the memory of how she came for me. How she came to my home and kissed me in the kitchen.

So, I lose my last inhibitions and my hand drifts down from her hair, along her neck, to her breast. I softly cup it and it doesn't feel untoward in the least. In fact, it feels like the most natural course of action in this moment. Yet doubt flickers in me as I wait for her reaction.

But Helen throws her head back, exposing her neck to me. An opportunity I eagerly take. I cup her breast a bit more firmly and kiss my way down from her mouth to her neck.

We're going to have to get out of the kitchen but I don't want to break the spell. Helen's right hand meanders downward as well. She looks at me while she lays it over my breast and gently squeezes, her thumb brushing over my rock-hard nipple.

"Bedroom?" she asks.

Wordlessly, I nod. I all but drag her out of the kitchen, through the lounge and into my bedroom. I briefly consider texting Jess to implore her not to come home any time soon, but there's no time for that. Knowing Jess, she'll give me all the space I need.

Helen doesn't even cast a glance at my room. She only has eyes for me. She comes for me again and I still can't believe it. It might only be for a brief time on a Sunday afternoon, but all my dreams are coming true. Professor Swift wants me. There are no two ways about it anymore.

"Is all of this okay with you?" she asks, suddenly. She's pressed all the way against me, her breath hot on my cheeks, so it's the last question I expected. I believed it was implied. But I understand her reasons for asking me so explicitly.

"It's more than okay." I give a little nod, to make sure there's no doubt about my intentions.

It's everything, I think to myself. To me, right now, it's absolutely everything.

"Good." She smiles for the first time since she set foot in my apartment.

I try to smile back but my lips want other things. They want to feel hers again. They want to explore her body. My brain can barely fathom the fact that she's in my bedroom, let alone that my lips might skate along her skin soon.

She wants me. I want her. This is going to happen.

I can feel my pulse all through my body. My desire for Helen beating in it. She's so beautiful. In the light of my room, her wavy blonde hair makes her look like an angel. An angel of lust sent to drive me crazy, but an angel nonetheless. I wonder what she's thinking when she looks at me like that. When she comes for me, like now. Her lips hover over mine again, but her upper body has left a little gap. She fills the gap by cupping my breast in her hand and a moan escapes my throat. It's caught by her wild mouth on mine. She's suddenly so ferocious and free. This isn't Professor Swift in my bedroom. This is another version of her. Or at least another side. A side I'm privileged to witness.

I give as good as I get because, somewhere in the back of my mind, despite the sanctity of this moment, a thought looms that this can only be a one-off. That Helen Swift will only once in her life come for me like this. After this is all over, she'll go back to being her professional, professorial self, and she won't allow herself to indulge in this temporary insanity again. My mind seems to be acutely aware of this and it's making my body want her even more.

She's wearing a pale yellow blouse and I go to work on the buttons. There's an urgency to my actions because I also fear she might put a stop to this at any time. Although, when we take a breather, the look in her eyes tells me she's not going anywhere soon.

There are a million things I want to ask her, but they'll have to wait, because Helen's hand slides from my breast to the hem of my top. She pushes herself away from me so she has room to hoist it over my head. Then I stand in front of her in just my bra. My skin breaks out in goosebumps and I resume my work on the buttons of her blouse. She helps me by pulling it out of her trousers and, when the buttons are undone, letting it slide off her arms.

She's wearing a run-of-the-mill white bra—she probably didn't plan for this—but, to me, it's the most exotic piece of lingerie ever created. I still want to peel it off her as quickly as possible, though.

Because we've passed the next threshold. We're at the next level of intimacy. Another barrier in our professor-student relationship has been broken down.

Then, she surprises me again by bringing her hands to her back and taking off her bra for me. Her skin is so pale and she suddenly looks fragile. I can see it reflected in her gaze as well. There's more uncertainty there where earlier it was brimming with confidence. She's literally laying herself bare for me and it tells me everything I need to know.

I mirror her actions and quickly dispose of my own bra.

"You're so incredibly beautiful," she says, and ever so gently, lays a hand on my chest.

"So are you," I whisper, pushing the words past the lump in my throat. This has gone from wild desire to something else very quickly. Something deeper, something that even shuts up the little voice in the back of my head insisting this is a one-off. Right now, it seems like much more than that. It seems like something I want to be doing for the rest of my life, and we're only half-naked.

Helen caresses my breast and my nipple stands to attention.

I watch her as she rolls it between her fingers. I watch her do this to me and it turns me on so much, I feel like I need to get the rest of my clothes off pronto. But I also know that I want to refer to her for what happens next. I can't explain why, but it's important that she set the pace. She came here; she kissed me. She hardly said a word. Now we're half-naked in my bedroom. This is Helen's show and I wouldn't want it any other way.

She looks into my eyes as she pinches my nipple again, a little harder now. She narrows her eyes and if it's still there, I can no longer see the insecurity in them. She looks like she's doing exactly what she wants to do—what she's been wanting to do for a while.

I don't know her all that well, but perhaps revealing to me that she's a writer equalled intimacy for her. It brought her close to me in a way neither one of us could have anticipated. It should have been clear when she returned my kiss last week. But it's so easy to misunderstand things in life. I'm over the moon that we seem to understand each other seamlessly now.

Then she surprises me again.

"Do you like that?" she asks, but it doesn't sound like a question. It sounds as though she knows very well how much I like it and she's revelling in my display of it. She's enjoying the power she has over me.

I nod because it's all I can do.

She brings her other hand to my other breast, making me a passive receiver of her affections. But only for a brief moment, I vow. She rolls both my nipples between her fingers and arrows of pleasure shoot through me. Between my legs, a strong beat pulses. Those fingers. Will they go to where my pulse is the fiercest? The thought alone is enough to elicit another moan from my throat.

"Oh, Rory," she groans in response. She slants towards me

HARPER BLISS

and kisses my exposed neck. Her hands remain on my breasts, her fingers on my nipples, and I feel my knees buckle.

When her lips find my mouth again, her breath on me is hot and ragged. Her hands meander down, to the button of my jeans. She flips it open and lets her hand skate inside for a split second. Her fingers there elevate the pulse between my legs to a wildly beating mess. To a drum symphony for her. One that only she can ever understand.

She pulls her head back and there's a grin on her lips. It's giving her a thrill to have me at her mercy like this. Her fingers only remain in my trousers for a few seconds, then she pulls them out and unzips my jeans. I help her push them down. My knickers are staying on for now and, for some reason, I'm glad. It's my last layer of protection against this mad lust. I want her so badly, I want to tear them off, but I don't want to surrender so easily either.

I make a move for her trousers, but she beats me to it. She slips out of them with quick ease and then nothing can stop me any longer. I walk us over to my bed. It's unmade and next to it lays my Kindle with the H.S. Barr book that I fell asleep to last night. H.S. Barr is in my room now. Last night, when I was reading her words, I could only dream of that ever being the case. Now, here she is.

I shove my duvet to the side until it tumbles off the bed, making room for us. I pull her down with me and then we lie face to face, only wearing knickers. If I believed we were intimate before, this has taken things to yet another level. To have Helen's near-naked body so incredibly close to me makes me break out in goosebumps all over again.

Her skin is impossibly pale all over, except for what looks like a birthmark on the outside of her upper thigh. I trace its contours with my finger. This is a moment to take a breath and to take in what we are doing. Her body is lean, almost wiry. Even when she's lying in bed with me like this, she still manages to look distinguished. It's all in her eyes, in those mysterious pools of grey-blue. I've never encountered this eye colour before, or if I have, it left my head the moment I met Helen Swift. I trace my finger up along her thigh, over her side, to her breast. I take it in my hand as though it's the most revered body part that ever existed. When she leans in to kiss me again, I can sense the desire in her and it drives my own up another notch. For Helen to want me like this is more than any fantasy I could ever have dreamed up.

Her lips lock onto mine, and my hand is pressed between our chests. This kiss is different. It starts slow and sultry but quickly transforms into something much more insistent. An exchange of intentions. There's no way back now.

I can't remember a time in my life when I was this aroused, when my skin vibrated with such heat and my body trembled with such desire. I'm not sure what it is about Helen that drives me so wild, and maybe it's the fact that I can't put my finger on it, that it's all so mysterious, that makes her so compelling. I don't know her. I don't know her motives—I can only guess at them. I'm not even sure why I kissed her last week, apart from that clear burst of desire that made me do it at the time. Put this up to scrutiny and what will remain? Pure lust—or something more?

Our kiss intensifies and so do our actions. The next moment, she's lying half on top of me, her delicious body stretched over mine. I can feel so much of her. She's soft in some places and hard in others—all places I want to explore in a different manner. Slowly and deliberately. Mapping them in my head so I never forget.

Helen kisses her way down my body. When I open my eyes, her face hovers over my breasts. Her lips are so close, my nipples want to reach up and touch them. I watch how her tongue flicks out of her mouth and she touches only the very tip to my nipple. I see it more than I feel it, that's how subtle, how quick and erratic, her touch is.

But it's the sight of her that drives me crazy more than anything else. That unleashes the real wetness between my legs. I'm so ready for her now. I want her with an intensity that is taking me over completely.

Her tongue grows more audacious and her licks along my nipple become longer, wetter, warmer. At the same time, her hand travels downward, between my legs. I spread them for her as wide as my current position allows.

As she sucks my nipple all the way into her mouth, her finger skates along the wet panel of my knickers. My clit is so pumped and ready for her, but her finger only skates along it briefly. Too briefly. My engine revs up some more. I push myself towards her to make the last of my intentions known. Those fingers. I want them inside me.

When Helen looks at me, I know she knows what I want. I may not know anything else, but I know that much. My desire must be plastered all over my face, it must be smouldering in my eyes. How does it make her feel? I try to gather it from the look in her eyes, but my attention is drawn elsewhere. Her fingers are once again between my legs, drawing circles around my aching clit.

I could come, I think. I could so easily come at the lightest touch of her fingertip. That's how much I want her, how much having her here has aroused me.

Even though her finger is rubbing very insistently along the panel of my knickers now, I still have trouble believing this is actually happening.

Helen's finger travels all the way up to the hem of my knickers and she hooks it underneath. I still have the presence of mind to help her slide them off—because never in my life have I wanted to get rid of a piece of clothing more than in this moment of aching lust.

All that came before matters, it matters so much, and it could come to mean so much in the future, yet it pales in comparison to the sensation of spreading my legs for Helen Swift. Of baring myself to her. Of having her look down at me, her gaze travelling from my eyes, over my breasts, to the place between my legs where I can feel my desire for her culminate.

Her gaze travels up again and she locks it on me. Her eyes are different. There's a softness in her gaze. There are flickers of pure lust. She keeps looking at me while her fingers touch down again, on the bare skin of my inner thighs first. She draws circles there, then draws closer to my pulsing clit.

I let out a gasp of air. Her gaze on me is almost too intense but it's also electrifying and dizzying and utterly intoxicating. This is no longer a mere teacher crush. This is so much more than that. In this moment, it's what every fibre of my being revolves around. There's only her. And me, wanting her so much I feel like I might explode out of my skin if she doesn't touch me where I want her to soon.

Then, she does. Her finger skates along my clit and I arch up towards her. She's no longer looking into my eyes. She's looking at what her finger is doing between my legs. I wish I could see it, but I don't have to see it to feel what it does to me.

It might be the worst mistake of my life, but I'm in love with Professor Swift. I know that in this moment better than I know anything else.

A fire is lit beneath my skin. It spreads across my body, leaving a tingling sensation in its wake. Her finger slides through my wetness. I glance at her because I need to see her reaction to my blatant lust for her.

Helen's mouth is slightly agape, as though she's in awe of what she's witnessing. As though she can't believe what the touch of her finger is evoking in me.

Her wet finger circles my clit and it's almost too much for me to bear. But I don't want this sensation to end. I will only surrender to her when I really can't take any more. Then her finger slides down again, between my wet folds, and she very, very slowly slips it inside. Just a fraction, but enough to make me gasp for air again.

My eyes have fallen shut but it's as though I can feel her gaze on me. When I open my eyes she's looking at me. Is that a grin on her lips? She knows she has me completely enthralled. My desperate gasp must have given me away.

Her finger moves but only ever so slightly, yet it feels as though the earth is shaking beneath me. She sends me one last grin, before shuffling down, bending towards my clit and flicking her tongue against it.

As she does, her finger slides in deeper, and I have no choice but to surrender.

Her finger slips back out a few moments later, and she adds a second one. Her tongue lavishes my clit with the most delicious flicks of attention.

I bring my hand down and grab hold of a fistful of her hair. Stars explode on the back of my eyelids. My surrender has come fast and strong. Sometimes, there's no choice. Not when Helen Swift is doing this to me.

Her fingers delve deep inside of me and touch me in a place that, perhaps, no one has ever touched me before. It's not a mere physical place. It's the point in my body where everything converges. My desire for her, my admiration, the chance I took when I kissed her. Even though my eyes are firmly closed now, I see her pale-blue gaze. I see that lovely smile she can paint on in a fraction of a second. And in the blackness behind my eyes, I know that smile is only meant for me.

"Oh, Helen," I groan, losing myself to her ministrations even more. Her tongue is warm and soft and insistent and her fingers are possessive and driving me firmly towards my inevitable climax.

When I come, I open my eyes wide, because I want to see. I

want to imprint this image in my memory forever. I only see my hand in her hair, the slant of her neck as she is bent towards me, but it's more than enough to make a lasting memory.

My limbs stiffen for an instant as I give myself to Helen completely. My orgasm is intensified by the prospect of me doing to her, in a matter of minutes, what she's just done to me. It seems so unreal and for a moment, I doubt it will even happen, but I know that it will. There's no choice.

She releases my clit first, but her fingers remain inside. Her chin glistens and it's truly a sight to behold. A sight I never thought I'd see.

I can't move or speak, I can only moan to utter my satisfaction. That grin is back on her face as she slips her fingers out of me. She seems mighty pleased with herself. I can't wait to wipe that grin off her lips.

31

HELEN

It feels as though I have Rory all over me. I can taste her on my tongue and my fingers are sticky with her wetness. I'm the most aroused I've been in years, perhaps decades. In fact, I don't recall ever feeling like this. Because the situation is so very peculiar.

I didn't come here to take Rory to bed. I didn't even come here to kiss her—not if my conscious mind had anything to do with it. Yet, look at me now.

Her hair is fanned out around her head as she lays panting, basking in her post-orgasmic glow. And she's really basking. She's the very definition of post-climax bliss. She has the most content smile on her face. I may not have a clue how I ended up in her bedroom, naked in her bed, because the sequence of events is not something I can process right now, but I can see for myself how happy Rory is with what has just transpired.

Strangely enough, I don't feel the urge to flee. I want to stay, not just because I'm so incredibly aroused right now I'm no longer sure of my ability to actually walk out of this bedroom, but because I genuinely want to stay with Rory. It seems, to my surprise, that she has that effect on me.

I press my body against hers and let my gaze wander over it again. Goodness, her body. Her smooth skin, unmarred by wrinkles or exposure to the elements. Before she took off her clothes, I had no idea it would entice me to such an extent that, even now, I can't keep my hands off her.

"That was amazing," she says. Her voice sounds different, like it has dropped an octave. God, it was divine to make her come.

I look into her eyes. They're so dark and warm. I could look into those eyes for a good while longer, but I suppose I should say something. I'm not sure what. My chest puffs up with something akin to pride, but I still don't know what to say. Instead, I kiss her. When I do, it occurs to me that I'll be fifty in a few months' time. Was buying a Porsche perhaps not enough? Is that the reason why I'm kissing Rory Carlisle like this, as though my very life depends on it? Or is there a different reason?

It doesn't really bear thinking about right now. It would spoil the moment and this is not a moment I want to spoil. I might not have one like this ever again in my life. Which is why I kiss her as though there's no tomorrow.

My hands roam towards her breasts again, but she nudges me away. She pushes until I'm on my back and her hands gently cup my breasts. She gazes down at me as if to say that she'll handle things from now on. Then I hear a sound coming from inside the apartment.

Is that the front door?

I freeze and so does Rory. Her roommate's home. Oh, damn.

Rory's lips curl into a smile but I don't think this is funny at all.

"It's just Jess," she says.

It's instantly very clear to me that Jess's arrival is my cue to leave. I'm brusquely snapped out of this... faux-pas—because that's what it has now become—and my level of arousal drops accordingly.

"I'd better go." I manoeuvre myself out from under her.

"No, Helen, wait," she pleads. "Let me just go talk to her. I'll ask her to leave."

She doesn't give me a chance to respond. In a flash, she has jumped off the bed and grabbed a robe from the back of the door.

"I'll only be a second, I promise." With that, she's out the door, closing it behind her.

What am I even doing here? The fact that Rory has a room-mate is what drives it home for me most. I should be with a woman who, at the very least, has her own space. Not a bloody student. What was I even thinking? I wasn't, which is clearly the issue here.

I hop out of bed and look around for my clothes. I need to get out of here. I need to get home. I've hardly done any work this weekend. I gather my clothes which brings me closer to the door, and I hear whispers coming from the other side.

"Swift is in there?" I hear someone say. That must be Jess. I know Jess, of course. Sarah's her supervisor. There's no way I can walk out of this room and out of this apartment as long as Jess is here. I can't make out the next whispers but I do hear some very girlish giggling, followed by the pitter-patter of quick footsteps, then the slam of the front door.

Rory walks back into the room with an apologetic smile on her face. It quickly fades when she sees I've put my bra back on while she was asking Jess to leave.

"Please don't go." Her voice almost breaks.

"Rory, I—"

She doesn't give me the chance to finish my sentence. She bridges the distance between us and puts her hands on my hips.

"Jess won't be coming back until late tonight. I made sure of that." She cocks her head. "If you stay, I think I can make it worth your while."

"She knows I'm here. I heard you talk to her." I shake my head. "It has made me come to my senses."

"I know it's a massive interruption." Rory doesn't let up. "But nothing we can't come back from." She leans in and kisses my neck. It's almost enough to make me change my mind and stay. *Almost.*

"No." I take a step back and Rory's hands slip off my hips. She suddenly stands there so forlorn. "I shouldn't even be here in the first place. This is utter madness, Rory. What we're doing here."

"Helen, don't do this. Don't start rationalising now. We were having such a lovely time." She takes a deep breath. "How about we go to your place? I'll follow you in my car. Whatever makes you feel more comfortable."

"This whole thing is... so uncomfortable. And inappropriate. It's just not right."

"It sure feels right to me." She doesn't come for me again. And I can't bridge the gap either. The distance is there, and it unexpectedly hurts me that we're in this stand-off, but I need to respect it. Either it hurts now or it does tonight, or next week. Or next month.

"I have to be the wiser one here. I realise that."

"Helen." Her voice is more forceful. "Don't do that. I understand that you don't want to jump straight back into bed with me, but can we at least talk? You can't just up and leave."

I very much can, I think, but only for a split second. It wouldn't be fair to just dash out. It would be rather cruel.

"Okay, let's talk. But let's get dressed first. And if you could point me in the direction of the bathroom, please?"

"Helen." She's the one to take a step closer again. If she keeps doing that, she might end up convincing me to stay. Instead of saying anything else, Rory kisses me on the cheek. "I need you to know, to fully realise, that I want this. I'm a consenting adult. I'm crazy about you. Smitten. I won't let you go that easily." She kisses me on the cheek again, a little closer to my mouth this time. "The bathroom's just across the hall."

"Thanks." For all the things I've just said, I find it hard to move away from her. "I'll be right out."

I wash my hands and face and when I look in the mirror, I barely recognise myself. My hair's all over the place and it's not the same Helen staring back at me that I saw in Alistair's mirror this morning. I've just slept with my student. Not technically a student, I repeat in my head. But it doesn't matter. I'm her supervisor, her advisor. I have to keep a professional distance.

I huff out a deep sigh. This is all Alistair and Jack's fault. For a brief moment, they made me believe this was possible. I was all too eager to believe it. But it's not. It might have worked for them, but I'm nothing like either of them. Now Rory's roommate knows as well. I'll need Rory to swear her to secrecy. Sarah could find out this way and that would be a disaster. I'd never hear the end of it. This could very well cost me my reputation. I might feel quite ambivalent about my professorship at the moment, that doesn't mean my reputation isn't still of the utmost importance to me.

When I finally make it out of the bedroom, Rory is fully dressed and waiting for me in the lounge. She looks so much more vulnerable than before, as though I've already hurt her. God, I don't want to hurt her, but, the two things I want are diametrically opposed.

32

RORY

As soon as Helen joins me in the lounge, I know I won't be able to make her stay. She has that impenetrable veneer all over her again. She's gone back to being Professor Swift. To the person who kicked me out of her house last Sunday.

But I won't give up that easily. I will fight for this. Because I saw how she looked at me. I saw how much she wanted me and to not fight for that would be something I'd regret for the rest of my life. I'm just not sure how to go about it yet. The way she's sitting, all prissy, I think my best bet would be to give her the space she obviously needs.

"Helen," I whisper. "You're sending so many mixed signals, it's making my head spin."

She looks around nervously. "Are you sure your roommate isn't coming back any time soon?"

"Positive." I shuffle in my seat. "Shall I put the kettle on?"

She shakes her head, probably to indicate that she won't be staying much longer. Or perhaps she's thinking about what happened the last time I made tea, not even an hour ago. The fact is, I have no idea what she's thinking.

"I'm so sorry, Rory. I don't know what came over me. I've been chatting to Alistair and Jack and they were egging me on and... some other things happened that made me think about you. I know I'm blowing hot and cold and it's hardly fair on you." She seems to relax a little. She leans back and slings one leg over the other. "How about we sleep on it. We have our weekly meeting tomorrow. We can talk then."

"You told Alistair that I kissed you?" I need to make sure that Alistair kept his promise and didn't tell Helen that I told him about the kiss first.

"He's Alistair." She shrugs. "He has a nose for this kind of thing. Do you know how he met his husband?"

I think Jess told me about it once, but it's not something that's at the forefront of my mind. Especially not in my current state. I shake my head.

"Jack was a professor and Alistair was a student." She draws up her eyebrows. "Sound familiar?" She even manages a smile. "He might be a little biased towards the... *situation*."

"Really?" I'm surprised I forgot about that. "Did they meet here at Oxford?"

"Gloucestershire. Jack had to resign, even though Alistair wasn't his student. He was just a student at the university. It was a big mess. I didn't know Alistair back then. I only met him when he started at the English Department at Oxford, but..."

"But they're still together." Maybe that's not the point Helen's trying to make, but it's what I choose to highlight in what she has just said.

"Well, yes, but it's not been an easy road. Jack's had a very successful second career, but he never returned to academia..."

"From what you've told me, you have your second career all lined up." I know I'm being cheeky, but this is the woman who just gave me an earth-shattering orgasm. I'm not going to play coy with her now.

"That's not what I mean." She locks her gaze on mine for a split second, then it skitters away again.

"I can sleep on this for many a night, I'll still want you."

"I get that." She sends me a small smile. "But you can't possibly think we can have any sort of future together."

"I'm not that focused on the future right now. Only on the present." I need to get my hands on her, if not today, then tomorrow. From the way I want her, you'd think that Jess's impromptu arrival had left me hanging. I'll need to have a word with Jess about coming home so early, but then again, I never expected Helen to stay such a long time. I can't really hold it against her.

"I don't have that luxury, I'm afraid." Helen rubs her palms on her trousers. Is she making to get up and leave? If I have any moves left, I have to deploy them now.

In my heart, I know it's inevitable that she'll leave, but I want to delay the moment as long as possible. I want to delay the feeling of utter dread I expect to come over me when she closes the door behind her.

I have no reply to the defeatist words she just uttered. All I know about Helen's life are the tiny morsels she has shared with me so far. So, I'm the one who gets up. I sit down again very close to her. It takes all my willpower to not just straddle her and cover her in kisses. But I have to respect that she pulled the plug on our passionate afternoon. We can't just pick up where we left off. I'll give her the night of sleep she needs, but not before I've done this.

I put my hand on her knee and give it a gentle squeeze. She doesn't flinch nor does she swat my hand away. That's something.

I turn toward her and look into her eyes. I go all soft inside again. She's by far the most beautiful woman I've ever known.

"I know you have to go," I whisper. "I do understand, but..."

I finish my thought by pressing my lips against her cheek again, on the same spot where I kissed her earlier. So achingly close to her lips, but far enough removed to be considered chaste by some people—of whom I'm not one. Even this tiny peck sets me alight again in my belly. That same fire that burned inside me earlier flickers up again, it comes roaring out of nowhere. But I need to find a way to restrain myself. So I do. I give her one last kiss on the cheek, just to make my intentions fully known in case there was any uncertainty left.

"Oh, Rory," she says. "I'm not made of stone, you know." She covers my hand with hers. "We'll talk more tomorrow, I promise."

Then I know I have to let her go, but what she has just said is enough. I can make it through the night with that. I can dull the dreadful ache of her leaving.

As soon as Helen's gone, I text Jess. Not to make her feel guilty for her interruption, but because I need someone to process with.

By the time she arrives home, I've reluctantly showered. I wanted to keep Helen's smell on my skin for a good while longer, but today is not the day I get to have everything I want. I got so much more than I could ever have dreamt of already. And I still have the sheets on my bed—the bed Helen Swift and I made love in. Although calling it *making love* is perhaps pushing it a bit too far.

"Victoria Carlisle," Jess says. "I had to walk along the canal all the way to Wolvercote to process what I walked in on earlier." She cocks her head. "Are you okay? She hasn't broken your heart yet, has she?"

We sit and I tell her how Helen kissed me and we ended up in the bedroom. I leave out the most salient details.

"Well fuck me. Swift fucked you." She slaps her palms on her knees. "What's it going to be next Sunday? Will you be moving in together?" She plasters a broad smile across her face.

"Alistair must have said something to her to make her want to come over..."

"We can ask him. I have his number. I can call him right now if you like."

"God, no. I don't want to embarrass Helen. She was already embarrassed enough by you coming home."

"I'm so sorry, Rory. I honestly thought she would have left. I don't know what I was thinking."

"You can't tell anyone, Jess. You have to promise me." I drink from the tea I made just before Jess arrived.

"You don't even have to ask me that. You know your secret's safe with me. So..." She cups her hands around her tea mug. "You have your Monday meeting tomorrow after you've both had a night to sleep on it. Then what?"

"I don't know." I shrug. "I haven't slept on it yet."

"What I mean is..." She pauses. "We can joke about this all we want and I can encourage you like any enthusiastic best friend would, but... do you think you might fall in love with her?" I don't get to see Serious Jess too often, but she has materialised now.

"Oh hell, I don't know." My words don't exactly echo my sentiments. I think I could fall in love with Helen rather easily, but I'm also quite sure where that would leave me in the end. "Even if I did, you know..." I shrug again.

"I guess that's what you have to find out," Jess says, and gives me what I think is an encouraging smile. It looks a bit funny on her.

"I have no way of finding out other than actually being with her, and being with her might make me fall in love with her more quickly than I would like." I hadn't thought about it like this yet. But it doesn't matter. I've only been really in love a few times in my life and had my heart broken in the process a few times as well. In the end, it was always worth it. I'm not out to protect my fragile heart. I'm out to make Helen like me as much as I like her.

But first, a good night's sleep.

33

HELEN

On the one hand, I feel too mortified to even call Alistair. To get what happened off my chest, and to tell him it's all his fault. He should have known better than to encourage me. Or perhaps he was just testing me. I'm usually someone who can resist temptation more easily than give into it. But that didn't work this time. If only Rory hadn't been at the restaurant. I would have just driven home after brunch and moved on. But she keeps popping up. As though destiny won't allow me to get her out of my head so easily. I'm going to have to work for it.

On the other hand, a small part of me feels more alive than when I left my house the day before. I hadn't wanted to go to Sarah's dinner party—I hadn't wanted to be the fifth wheel once again.

For a brief moment, I allow myself to imagine what it would be like if Rory and I were together—and she was my plus-one for dinner parties. I could never introduce her to my friends the way Sarah did with Joan. It just wouldn't work. It's unthinkable. So there you have it. That's a lid on my imagination right there.

Yet, it was such a thrill to meet her—and to kiss. To end up in bed with her. I wonder what makes her so special? I've never shown the slightest proclivity towards women who are so much younger than me, let alone students. It has simply never occurred to me. Not even when I've seen it happen to colleagues or when Alistair told me how he met Jack. Because it's not how things are supposed to be—not in my world. I prefer to stick to the rules and I've never had any problems doing so, yet Rory is making it very hard. And I can't help but wonder why. Why her? Is it perhaps one of those predicaments in life that defies logical explanation?

I've studied English Literature all my life. I know all the ways in which silly—or not so silly—infatuation has been described and explained. Yet I feel as though none of that could ever apply to me. Maybe that's the silliest thing of all.

I spend the drive back to Upper Chewford in silence. I don't turn on the radio and I certainly don't dictate. I've completely forgotten where I am in my current work in progress. This isn't helping anything, really. And when I arrive home in a few moments, my bed will still be empty. Tomorrow, another work week begins and I can't afford to have Rory on my mind, occupying all the space there.

I scoff at myself at the impossibility of that because of our meeting tomorrow. I try not to think of Rory for the rest of the drive home, but even that proves impossible. Of course it does.

In the end, I turn on the radio as loud as I can bear it, just to drown out my own persistent thoughts of her naked body.

I had to force myself to eat lunch, but I'm regretting that now, as I wait for three o'clock to roll around. For Rory to knock on my office door. Even though we're having a regular, weekly student-supervisor meeting, it feels like something else entirely. Especially because I'm the one who promised that we would talk more today. After we'd both slept on it.

I did sleep on it and she was the first thing I thought about this morning. I managed to get some dictation done during my commute, but nowhere near as much as usual. Because sleep did not bring me a much-needed flash of wisdom on how to deal with this. I know what I *should* do. I know it all too well. The problem is that I don't feel much inclination towards doing it. Towards telling her that it's still very early in her research and she could still find another supervisor. I could even help her find one. Sarah could probably be persuaded to do it and would be a better fit than Alistair. But just the mere thought of Sarah giving Rory advice makes me jealous as hell.

But I know that's what I should do. Break all contact and move on. Maybe I could grab the opportunity to scale back my hours. See it as the sign I've been waiting for. A temporary interruption of my focus that has brought me to the other side stronger and wiser. But I don't feel wise, or strong. I just feel like I want to kiss her again.

Then the knock comes on my door.

"Yes." My voice sounds hoarse.

Rory walks in and it's as though the light in my office changes. As though her mere presence in this room changes the entire aspect of it. Makes the beige wallpaper flicker as though the most divine light has been cast upon it.

I'll need to snap out of this soon.

She sits without me having given her permission. Boundaries have been crossed. Chief among them is the one I obliterated when I ended up in her bed yesterday afternoon.

I wonder where the time has gone since then. The hours that have passed seem suddenly to have been compressed into this moment, and all the emotions I've had during them as well.

When I look at her, I have no desire whatsoever to ask her to find a new supervisor. I have the opposite of that desire. Or no, because, quite frankly, I don't much care about Rory's dissertation at this point, and that is perhaps my gravest fault of all.

I look away from her to regain some clarity. My gaze falls on a picture of all the members of the Oxford English Faculty, taken a few years ago. Yes, that should do the trick. Whenever I'm in trouble, I'll just focus on that to remind myself of my job and to forget about this errant lust coursing through me.

"Helen?" Rory leans towards the table. "Are you all right?"

I haven't said anything yet. My throat feels too dry to speak. It's like I've reached a vital crossroads in my life and my career. So much hinges on whatever I say next.

I look at her and take her in. She looks so fresh-faced, so blissfully youthful, innocent almost—although I know she is far from innocent. My gaze is drawn to her lips again. Oh, what I want those lips to do to me.

Instead of speaking, I get up. I swallow hard as I walk over to her. I tower over her and, inside of me, because of her intoxicating proximity, a warm feeling bursts open and spreads like a delicious glow beneath my skin.

"You must have put some sort of spell on me," I whisper. Then I lean towards her. Before I allow my lips to land on hers, again, I breathe in deeply. Just to take a moment. Perhaps to be able to excuse myself more easily after the fact—to tell myself that I did, in fact, take a moment. Not that it makes any difference whatsoever. Nor does it change my desire to kiss her.

I gaze into her eyes as she looks at me. I'm not doing this guilt-free. I'm well aware that kissing Rory in my office is another step on this path to someone I'm not, to someone I hardly recognise. This kiss will come at a cost, that much I know, but no cost great enough can hold me back.

She's the one who reaches out. She places her hand on my

cheek and pulls me closer. But I'm the one who kisses her. I'm the one who takes the action. I did so yesterday and I'm doing it again today. I should really lock the door, but the thought of someone knocking unexpectedly sends a whole new kind of shiver up my spine.

I kiss her and all sounds are drowned out. I close my eyes and the sensation of her tongue dancing with mine intensifies a millionfold. I hear nothing but the sounds our lips make and the soft, irresistible moans that escape her mouth, that drift into mine, that make me want her so much.

"You slept on it then?" Rory says, her voice not free of cheekiness, when our lips part.

"Hm," is all I can say.

She bursts into a giggle.

I crash into the other chair while shaking my head. "I should be able to resist you." I pin my gaze on her as though she's the guilty party here. "I forgive everyone I've called foolish and utterly ridiculous for feeling this way when they approached fifty." I throw my hands in the air.

"That's not what this is," Rory says, her tone suddenly serious.

"What is it then?" I sound incredulous, maybe too much so. But I can't tell her how I feel. I've shown her, but it's only the tip of the iceberg, only a tiny fraction of this desire pooling inside me. As though all the desire I never allowed myself to feel since breaking up with Sarah is catching up with me now and is all geared toward Rory.

"I want to kiss you and you, clearly, want to kiss me." She gives a quick shrug. "It makes us feel good and alive and..." She pushes herself out of the chair. "Makes us want to do it over and over again." She kisses *me* now.

Her lips touch against mine and my mouth opens with an eagerness I don't recognise in myself. It's as though I didn't just kiss her moments ago. I can't remember being like this with Sarah—maybe because she didn't allow me to be like this. It was all so measured and tainted by how she felt about herself. With Rory, her desire for me radiates from her every pore. I'm drawn to her carelessness and her fierceness. I want a piece of it.

She somehow manages to squeeze her knees either side of my legs and straddles me.

I place my hands on her back first, but it doesn't take long before they travel to her front, to her breasts, which I want to see naked again. I want Rory naked. I want her all over me again like yesterday. I want to finish what we started in her bed yesterday afternoon. With my eyes closed and her lips on mine, her tongue swirling in my mouth, I'm easily transported back to when I was licking her, tasting her...

I stop kissing her and pull my face back.

"We need to get out of here." I can't invite her into the tiny bedroom next to my office. I don't want to. We can't go back to her place with her roommate with the unfortunate timing.

She nods breathlessly.

"Shall we go on a trip to Upper Chewford?" It's the only place where we can do this properly. And who knows, I might even get her out of my system, although I sincerely doubt that.

She nods again. She doesn't look as though she minds the drive.

"I can leave here around four, but you should take your own car."

"Okay. I'll see you at your house at five then." The way she says it makes me think it will be a very impatient drive home, with no dictation done at all, unless my fictional detective all of a sudden lands herself in the most torrid sex scene.

She manoeuvres herself off me and straightens her clothing.

"Should I bring anything?" She stands there grinning at me.

It's her self-assuredness, I think. It's how she seems

completely comfortable with who she is even at such a young age—despite how her family feel about her being a lesbian.

"Just yourself."

"Okay." She lets her tongue flick over her lips.

"Okay," I echo, as though I still need some convincing. I don't.

She picks her bag off the floor and exits my office.

34

RORY

When I arrive in Helen's street, her car's not there yet. It's only half past four, but I couldn't wait any longer. I suppose I could go into the pub but I deem it too risky. Someone who knows my family might be there and ask me what I'm doing at The Golden Fleece on a Monday afternoon. I don't want to have to worry about that. I just want to think about all the things I want to do to Helen.

I hadn't expected her to kiss me today. I hadn't expected her to kiss me yesterday either. And that climax. It was so much more than just an orgasm. To me, it was an intention.

Jess's question still lingers on my mind as well. Could I fall in love with her? Of course, I could. I probably already am. It's brewing somewhere inside me, waiting for the right moment to wash over me.

Right now, I just want to be with her. I want her to look at me the way she did when I walked into her office earlier. That look, even more so than the subsequent kiss, told me—utterly convinced me—that she feels the same way. She can't hide it. There's something between us and we can't just deny it, we can't ignore it just because she's my supervisor. A feeling like this is way too precious. I think Helen realises that as well. Either way, I'm not backing off now.

I see a car turn into the street, but it's not her navy-blue Porsche. I would never have taken Helen for someone who'd buy such an ostentatious car, but then again, I don't know her all that well. I hope to get to know her a little better tonight.

I check my phone to see if she hasn't left any messages. It's probably a bit premature to text Jess that I might not be home tonight. I don't want to jinx things. And this is all so very unpredictable. Every time I think Helen's going to do something—or not do something—she goes and does the opposite.

Another car pulls into the street. Oh yes. Her Porsche is easily recognisable. It's not even ten to five. She's early. Maybe she couldn't wait. I know exactly how she feels.

As soon as she has parked, I hop out of my car. The sound of my door slamming shut draws her gaze to me. She doesn't smile, just gives me the most imperceptible of nods. I hurry to her front door and, without saying anything, she lets me in.

Part of me was worried she would change her mind. But she has that look on her face again, the one that makes me think I might be God's gift to professors on the brink of fifty. I can't suppress a smile.

"What's so funny?" she asks, as she pushes me against the front door. We haven't even properly made it into the house yet.

"Nothing," I whisper and pull her to me. Absolutely nothing, I think, when our lips meet again and again.

"Did you want some tea or anything else?" she asks, when, out of breath already, we break from the kiss.

"I want something." I look her straight in the eye. They're darker when she stares back at me, full of life and lust. It reminds me of how she looked at me yesterday when her finger slipped inside me. When she was driving me so wild that I could have come a thousand times over.

"I can guess what that is." She takes my hand and leads me up the stairs. No tea. No chat. Truth be told, I could probably do with a stiff drink right about now. I want this so much, it's making me jittery.

As I follow her, I take a few deep breaths and tell myself to just go with the flow. She might be a professor but this is not an exam.

I have no eye for the decor of her bedroom. I did catch a glimpse of her study on the way in. It reminds me of those books she still hasn't signed for me. Maybe without those books, I wouldn't be here today. It also reminds me of my father's old adage: always be reading a book, Rory. I've read all of Helen's books. I'm about to hop into bed with their author.

She comes for me hard—the same way she did yesterday. Maybe Helen Swift is simply a very passionate person behind those icy-blue eyes of hers. Or maybe this lust is of an intensity that only the two of us can share.

She takes a moment and looks at me again. I look back. She's not wearing her jacket anymore. When did she find the opportunity to take it off? I was so caught up in my lust for her, I didn't even notice.

She's wearing a white silk blouse that hangs loosely on her long frame. I want it gone as well. I vividly remember how surprised I was by her body yesterday. Its almost opaque paleness, but even more so, its surprising firmness.

When I took her to bed, it didn't feel as though I was sleeping with someone almost double my age. It, very simply, was making love to someone I wanted to make love to more than anything else. That same intense desire is building inside me now. All yesterday's emotions and sensations plus the added anticipation of today. And today, there are no more doubts. There's no roommate who can come home inconveniently. There's just Helen and me. And the electricity in the air between us.

❧ 35 ❧

HELEN

I know I'm the one who invited Rory over. The words still echo in my head—my brain seemingly devoid of anything else. Still, it's hard to believe this is about to happen. Everything that has happened thus far has been hard to believe. Sometimes, like now, I have to pinch myself to remind myself that this is really happening.

To think I brushed this off as a silly teacher crush, a youthful infatuation on her part. The way I feel right now, ablaze with lust, ready to pounce on Rory—again—it feels more like my very own silly infatuation. But it feels inevitable, more than something that's quickly getting way out of hand.

Even though I could have avoided this at several points in the past few weeks, there's a clear reason why I didn't. Things like this always happen for a reason. It's not just desire, although desire has the upper hand right now. It's something else. But whatever that something else is, it will have to wait to be analysed until later.

I want to do all the things I did to her yesterday again and again, and then some.

How is it even possible for someone to look so scrumptious

in just jeans and a jumper? Rory couldn't look more like a student if she tried. But she's not a mere student. She's the one who got through somehow. The one who's making me forget about all the things I *ought* to be doing and has me focusing instead on what I want to be doing.

I sit on the bed and beckon her.

With a confident smile on her face, she walks over to me. She places her legs on either side of my knees and wraps her arms around my neck. I arch myself up towards her. My hands travel underneath her jumper, up the skin of her back. It's so incredibly soft against my hands.

"Thanks for coming all this way," I say.

"You've already made it worth my while." She plants a soft kiss on the tip of my nose then looks at me again.

I smile back up her. My hands have wandered to the clasp of her bra. I unfasten it without further ado, then let my hands slip inside the cups. I'm still looking into her eyes when I take her breasts in my hands. I love the subtle shift in her expression. Her mouth opens slightly while her eyes narrow a fraction.

She pushes herself against my hands. I feel her fingers in my hair. She sinks her teeth into her bottom lip and regards me more intently.

She leans towards me and finds my ear with her lips. "I'm going to fuck you now, Helen. It's why I came here." Her words send a jolt of lightning straight to my clit. The audacity of them. This may be one of the reasons I want her so much. There's a boldness to her I've never encountered in a woman my own age. Not that I think it's a matter of age alone. The kind of women I've been with in the past might have something to do with it as well.

I cup my hands over her breasts more insistently, pinching her nipples between my fingers. Now that I've gotten over the shock of her saying those words, what she intended with them is fine with me. I think she knows that very well.

She pushes me down on the bed and stands over me. She hoists her jumper and bra over her head and tosses them into the room somewhere. The sight of her lights me up again—and my body already feels as though it's on fire. I reach for her breasts again—I think I might be cultivating a fetish—but she leans back. She won't let me touch them. A grin spreads on her lips. She goes for my trousers next. She unzips me and, swiftly, rolls them down my legs, tugging off my shoes in the process.

She really meant what she said then. She's not just going to fuck me. She's going to do it with a certain air of authority. God, the brashness of youth. There are so many things to like about Rory Carlisle and that's just another one of them in the long list of things I've already come to adore about her. On my way back from Oxford yesterday, I detoured past the Carlisle Manor, which isn't on my route at all. I'm rather intrigued by that as well.

She comes for my blouse next. She has to lean closer to me though and I can't help myself, even though I'm not making her job of undressing me very easy. Undressing can be such an awkward kerfuffle. I might as well make it a bit more fun by lunging for her breasts again. They're so perfectly shaped, at least from this angle. Or maybe they're not but that's how I see them. That's how I see *her*.

She pulls away again and reaches out her hand to me. I let her pull me up and my blouse and bra are disposed of in the same swift manner. Her hurry brings my lust to the surface.

Then she has me on the bed in just my knickers. She steps out of her remaining clothes. Oh Christ. Has she forgotten I'm a lady of a certain age? This might arouse me to the point of a heart attack. At the very least, I can feel my heart slamming itself against my breastbone—and every frantic beat is for her.

She joins me on the bed, pressing her body against my side, her hand hovering over my chest. With that Rory grin on her face, she glances at me, while she feigns touching her hand down on my breast. Her hand nearly lands, then retreats a few times, while her grin grows bolder. Her teasing doesn't miss its effect. It's not only my heart pulsing frantically now. It's all of me, and all of me seems to be compressed into a point between my legs. Oh, how I hope she'll keep her word soon. It doesn't look like she will, though. She looks so composed. The complete opposite of how frantically aroused I feel. How is this even possible? She seemed in such a hurry to undress me mere minutes ago.

Her fingers finally caress my breast. Her touch on my nipple is so light, I can barely feel it, yet it's though it's all I've ever felt in my life. The desire she sparks leaves me so utterly focused on her touch. Then, the light touch of her finger is replaced by the warm softness of her mouth.

"Oh, Rory," I moan. I press my fingertips against the flesh of her back. I can feel her hard nipples pressed against my side. Her tongue flicking over my own nipples sends me into the stratosphere already.

She releases my nipple from her mouth, looks me in the eye briefly, then bestows the same attention on my other one. This time, she takes it gently between her teeth and pulls at it.

My skin breaks out in goosebumps. What is this girl doing to me? What has she been doing all along? I can't even remember the day we met. She was just another student. No one special. How did that change so drastically?

I glance down at her, at her dark hair as she clenches her teeth around my nipple. Harder now. More insistent, but still as unhurried as before. We have the rest of the day to do this. The thought fills me with a sense of calm I was missing yesterday, but it doesn't quench the urgency I feel in my gut.

She slips on top of me, her knee pushing between my legs. I want to push myself against her. For an instant I think of stopping myself from doing so, but I have no reason to stop. Rory is completely uninhibited. With her, today, I can let go. I can do whatever I want. So I do.

I press myself against her upper thigh. My clit is so sensitive, I never want to pull away, that's how good it feels.

"Rory," I say, my voice pleading. "Fuck me now. Just fuck me now." I barely recognise the sound of my own voice. Helen Swift would never dream of uttering such words, yet I was the one who just spoke them. Maybe it's my alter ego, H.S. Barr. But she's usually just as uptight as I am.

She grins at me again. "Patience, Professor," she says.

"You can tease me all night long, but... I've waited long enough," I remind her. It feels as though part of the arousal we built up to yesterday hasn't left my body yet. It reignited in full force the moment she wrapped her lips around my nipple.

"All night long, eh," she says and nods.

I guess I'll be wanting her—needing her—to stay. I might as well keep her near now that I can. Now that we are ensconced in the privacy of my home. God knows how either of us will feel about this in the morning.

I nod back.

In response, she pushes her thigh harder against me.

"Technically, you are sort of my boss," she says, and leans in close to my ear again. "So I'd better do as you tell me." She kisses my neck, slowly, slowly, as though she has no intention of honouring my request any time soon at all. But her thigh is still pressing against me and it's enough, for now, to tide me over until she, finally, gets around to peeling my knickers off me.

She kisses me on the lips. Our mouths are now already so familiar with each other. She tugs at my bottom lip with her teeth while looking me in the eye. And I can see it now. I can see in her eyes what this means to her. The grin she greeted me with earlier seems long gone. There's no more teasing. This is serious business now.

She kisses her way down—all the way down. Until she's

huddled between my legs. I can see her examining my knickers as though considering what to do with them. She leans in and kisses the skin above the band. They're the most daintiest of kisses, yet they set my skin on fire.

She traces a path down with her lips and tongue. She kisses the fabric of my knickers over my clit, sending wave after wave of hot fire through my body.

Oh Christ. She really does mean business. I feel her tongue all wet and soft through my knickers and while the last barrier between us is something I'd like to get rid of as quickly as possible—to feel the full force of intimacy that the direct touch of her tongue on me there will create—it's also the last barrier protecting the Helen I was before I met Rory. Before I let her into my life, into my house, and into my bedroom. Because this is the most extraordinary behaviour I've engaged in in my entire life. Finding my true calling as a cozy crime writer has nothing on this. Having this woman in my bed—between my legs—is so much more. She's erasing parts of me I've clung to for such a long time just by being here, by doing what she's doing this very instant.

Finally, she pushes my knickers to the side, exposing me to the air—and her gaze. This is no time for mid-life related self-esteem issues—I bought a Porsche to deal with those—but I do wonder, if only for a split second, what it's like for her to be in bed with me.

I only have to catch a glimpse of her face, of the sheer desire in her eyes, to be convinced of her lust for me. I can fail to understand it, perhaps, but I can't fail to notice it.

She looks me in the eye briefly. She licks her lips. My entire body is throbbing, trembling while it waits for her touch. As she returns her focus to my pulsing clit, I wonder what will happen with Rory and me.

Then I stop wondering anything at all because her tongue is

all over me. She licks along my lips and sucks my clit into her mouth and it sends my body into blissful overdrive.

It's not the fact that I have missed this in my life, the kind of intimacy that can only be reached with someone I truly care about—and I do care about her, a lot—it's the trajectory that has brought us here.

My mind goes blank. I've been waiting for this. I never knew I was waiting for someone like Rory but I do know now, as I start shuddering towards my inevitable climax. I know it in my bones that I will never be the same after this.

The orgasm shakes me to the core. It leaves me breathless and raw and, for a moment, I feel so very exposed. So naked, not just my body but my entire emotional world.

When she snuggles up to me I can't immediately utter any words that make sense, so I pull her close, as though I never want to let go of her again. Maybe I don't.

"What have you done to me?" I say, after a while.

She replies by wrapping her arms around me more tightly and kissing me fully on the lips.

❧ 36 ❧

RORY

"I don't have much in the house," Helen says. "I hadn't planned on a dinner guest."

We've gone downstairs to catch our breath and drink some much-needed water. Helen's wearing nothing more than a robe, while I've slipped into my jeans and jumper, totally commando. In my frenzy to get here—and not wanting to seem too presumptuous—I didn't pack any spare underwear or clothes.

"I can call George. Ask him to bring some food." I pull my legs up to have something to throw my arms around.

Helen chuckles. "What's it like growing up with a butler?" She looks in the fridge but turns back to me with a shrug. "Sorry, H.S. Barr made a domestic non-goddess out of me."

"An undomesticated mere mortal without a butler." I take a few sips of water. "What on earth have I got myself into?"

"I usually stop by the shop on my way home on Mondays, but a member of the local aristocracy made me sway from my routine."

"Minor aristocracy, and I'm really not very hungry." I want to get up and walk over to her. Making Helen climax was, without a doubt, the single most supreme moment of my life.

The way she threw her head back and called my name. I can't wait to experience it again. One single hit of that and I'm addicted.

She sits down at the table with me. "You didn't answer my question." She looks at me with a grin on her lips. "Did the butler do everything for you? When was the first time you set foot in a grocery shop?"

"I can't really remember my first time." I chuckle at the notion she has of me and my life. "It was so long ago."

"Fair point."

"Were you being serious earlier when you said we had all night?" Helen has her guard down so I might as well ask her now. I have been asked to leave rather abruptly before.

"I have zero incentive to kick you out of my house." She leans over the table and grabs my hand. "On the contrary."

"Good. I really should spend more time in Upper Chewford. This is my hometown, after all."

"I haven't had someone stay over in a very long time."

"Then I'm honoured." Not only that, I'm elated too. I remember when Jess suggested that this might not be impossible. That something might actually happen between Helen and me, and how utterly ludicrous I considered the notion. And look at me now. Drinking water at her kitchen table to quench my thirst after making love.

"Good. Honour will have to do, seeing as I can't provide sustenance."

I do get up and walk over to her now. "I have all the sustenance I need," I say, as I stand behind her and wrap my arms around her. I don't care if it sounds sappy. The feeling of her body against mine ignites something in me again, something that's been dormant for too long.

"Let's go into the lounge." Helen leans against me. "It's more comfortable."

I kiss her briefly on the skin of her neck, then head into the lounge with her. My gaze lands on her bookshelves.

"Can I get my signed H.S. Barr books now?"

"I suppose you've worked hard enough for them." She sits and pulls me down next to her.

"I believe I have paid for at least one in kind." I lie with my head in her lap. "I intend to pay for the other two before the sun rises in the morning."

She smiles down at me. "I have a new one coming out soon."

I nod, pushing her robe open with the movement of my head. "How about I pay you in advance for that one as well."

"Thank you." A more serious note has crept into her voice. "For reacting the way you did when I told you about my writing. Not many Oxford English Literature students would respond to the news that way." She narrows her eyes. "Unless… you only said those things—"

I shake my head so vigorously my cheek touches her naked thigh. I can smell her earlier arousal. Or perhaps it has been renewed already.

"I read all three of your books, the first one before I even knew it was yours. I finished the third one yesterday. You're a great writer, Helen. And this is a true double whammy for me."

She runs her hand through my hair. "Who knew minor aristocracy could be so charming."

"I slept with Helen Swift *and* H.S. Barr."

"You're the first to do so."

My eyes grow wide. "You haven't… been with anyone since you started writing?" I look into her gorgeous eyes.

"Where would I have found the time?"

"I hope I'm not keeping you from more important tasks."

"Nothing's more important than this right now." She leans down and kisses me on the forehead.

When I wake up, I'm utterly famished. Then I look at Helen and my hunger disappears. She's still asleep and I make the most of the opportunity to observe her features undisturbed. She looks more peaceful than I've ever seen her, which is no surprise. What is this doing to her? What does she really think about me?

We spent most of last night bantering and exploring much more of each other's bodies—each moment creating a memory of pure joy. But can this ever be more than the memories we've created?

She looks so different with her eyes closed, without her inquisitive blue gaze on me. I notice a few very faint freckles next to her nose. Her hair is fanned wildly around her head, covering most of the pillow.

A small part of me wonders if she'll kick me out as soon as she wakes. But I did everything she asked of me. I even fucked her when she asked me to.

Then the urge is too strong and I run a finger over her upper arm. Not to wake her—because I could look at her like this forever—but just to feel her skin against mine again.

Her eyes flutter open slowly. She blinks a few times as though she can't quite get me into focus.

"Hey." Her voice is barely audible.

"Hi." I kiss her on the arm where my finger just caressed her. "Did you get some sleep?"

"Not much." She stretches her arms above her head and her face scrunches up in the cutest way. "I blame you."

"I take full responsibility." I snuggle up to her. "You should see fit to discipline me in any way you deem appropriate," I whisper in her ear.

"Good." She pulls me close. "Your punishment is taking responsibility for all of this." I can feel her sigh against the skin of my neck. "If only it were that simple." She presses a soft kiss to my cheek. "Do we really have to get up and face the world?"

"We can elope to my family's house in Scotland if you like." I turn to her. "You can write and I can do my research remotely."

"What will your family have to say about that?" Helen plays along and, even though it's just a silly fantasy, it fills me with joy.

"I'll tell Mother I hired my supervisor to live in with me. She believes in hiring people, so that should keep her quiet for a while." I chuckle.

"So... I would be your staff?"

"Well, I would see you more as..." I run a fingertip across her spine. "My sex slave." I burst into a full fit of giggles. Then my stomach grumbles loudly.

"As long as you don't ask me to fulfil too many domestic duties." Helen smiles, then puts a hand on my belly. "I must feed you now. To have you fast any longer would be negligent."

"We'll have to go out." I scan her face for a reaction.

"I'll quickly pop into the coffee shop and grab us something." She pulls away from me.

"Can I come with you?"

She grimaces. "This is a small village and you may think you don't know anyone here, but people do know you. They know your family. If we walk to the village square together on a Tuesday morning, there will be instant chatter and it will raise too many unnecessary questions."

I nod my understanding. "What time do you have to be at the university?"

She falls back onto the pillow with a sigh. "I'm not teaching this morning, thank goodness. I have a few meetings this afternoon." She turns to me. "I can linger a little." She looks me in the eye. There's something in her glance that wasn't there before. A hint of reality. Helen ignores reality for a few more seconds and kisses me on the lips. "We should probably talk," she says, after she pulls away again. "But first... food!"

37

HELEN

After a quick shower, I leave Rory alone in my home—an odd feeling in addition to the many others I've had since inviting her over, again—and head to the village square.

If only we could walk around Upper Chewford together. If only she wasn't a student. If only she wasn't twenty-two years younger than me.

Ironically, Upper Chewford is the only place Sarah ever wanted to walk around hand-in-hand with me. I guess I can only now see her point of view, her desire to keep things hidden. I used to give her such a hard time about her self-loathing. Now it feels like I'm on my very own walk of shame.

It's not far to the village square where I opt to go to the bakery instead of into the coffee shop. I buy a loaf of bread and a couple of croissants. I have no idea what Rory likes for breakfast. I'm sure some toast will do.

I hurry back home but relish the opportunity to take a few deep breaths on my way back. Because it's a work day, I only encounter a few people and with all three of them a nod suffices. I try to imagine what it would be like to walk the streets of Upper Chewford with Rory by my side. I get an instant vision of her mother storming up to us, asking me what on earth I'm doing with her daughter.

I try to shake off the thought but it's not easy because this is the exact question I'm asking myself. What am I doing with Rory?

I haven't a clue.

When I reach my street, I pull up my collar a little higher, as though it can protect me from any unwanted stares. I've almost made it to my house, when Stacey opens her door and jumps out.

"Helen," she half-whispers. "Is that the Carlisle girl's car parked in the street? I saw her arrive last night. Is she—"

"No, Stacey." I try to cut her off before I have to make up any more lies. "Just one of my students who's in a spot of bother. Nothing to worry about." On the inside, I'm fuming at her nosiness. It's nine o'clock in the morning and she's already accosting me.

"I'm sorry things didn't work out with Mireille," she says. "She told me about what's-her-name."

"Don't worry about it." I put my key in the lock. "I have to get going now. I have work."

"Of course." She looks at me as though she knows very well I misled her about Rory's identity. "Have a lovely day, Helen."

Fat chance of that, I think, as I enter the house. It smells of freshly brewed coffee which is not something I'm used to coming home to.

I find Rory in the kitchen. She's showered and dressed. She has laid the table and beams me a wide smile. How am I going to tell her that this is impossible? That we can't meet at her place or at mine. That this probably should never have happened. That I was the one who failed to take responsibility. *This* will be her punishment in the end. I hate to be the one to inflict it on her, but what choice do I have?

"Coffee?" she asks, as though she's been making coffee in my kitchen all her life.

"Sure." I buy myself some time by taking condiments out of the fridge and dropping slices of bread into the toaster.

When I finally sit down, I'm so hungry, I can't have this chat with her before I've eaten something. We have worked up quite the appetite since yesterday afternoon. It's the first time we share a meal together and I can't help but notice her impeccable table manners. I don't think I've ever seen someone spread jam on a piece of toast so daintily.

"Did you manage to fly under the radar?" She fixes me with a stare. She's taunting me. Maybe she knows what's coming.

"Not really. Apparently my neighbour recognised you."

"The one who accosted you when I came here the first time?" She frowns. "Does she have nothing better to do than to watch you come home every single time? Or does she have a secret crush on you?"

I roll my eyes. "The first option."

"She recognised me as what?"

"A Carlisle."

Rory chuckles. "You'd think we were famous around these parts."

"To some people, you very much are."

Rory shakes her head. "But I haven't lived here in so long and even when I did, I hardly ever came into the village." She bites a tiny chunk of her toast and chews it slowly. "What did you tell her?"

"That you're not who she thinks you are." It sounds so silly now. So ridiculously cloak-and-dagger.

Rory sniggers. "Jesus." She looks at the remains of her slice of toast. "Goodness, toast has never tasted so good."

Once I've satisfied my most urgent hunger and need for

HARPER BLISS

caffeine, I lean against the back of my chair. I let Rory finish
her meal. I'm buying myself time. I don't want her to go. I don't
want this to end. It has barely even begun. But last night was so
much more than that first kiss we shared. I should have been
stronger then. At least when she kissed me, I had the excuse of
her saying all those kind things to me about being a writer.
Now, I have no more excuses left. Only my desire for her.
Which is not something I should act upon any further.

"As I said earlier." She has finished her second slice of toast.
"We should talk."

She nods. "I know what you're going to say, Helen." She
looks away. "You don't have to say it."

"But, I—" I don't know how to reply to that.

"You want me, I know that much," Rory says. "But you feel
like you can't have me, because you're a professor and I'm a
DPhil student. Because you feel like your neighbour is already
on to us. Because... I'm sure there are many other reasons."

I should thank her for saying the words I probably wouldn't
have been able to utter. For being the wiser one. For taking
responsibility.

"But tell me this..." She crosses her arms in front of her
chest. "How will you stop yourself from kissing me when you
see me next?"

I take a few moments to reflect. It's a very pertinent question. "Maybe..." I'm glad I only had one slice of toast because
the imminent sadness is already contracting my stomach. "It
would be best if you found another supervisor."

Rory's face tenses. I can hardly look at her. After the night
we had, the intimacy we shared, and the sheer joy of it when we
took reality from the equation, it's so difficult to have to say
this. But in a way, it was always implied. No promises were
made. A kiss is not a promise, nor are the orgasms she provided.
They only exist in the vacuum we created, behind the closed

214

door of my house. But behind that door, the real world lurks, and the real world has no place for us together.

"Sure." Rory's tone has grown cold. Hard. As though her heart has turned to stone. "That's what I'll do then." She pushes her chair back. She casts me one last glance and heads out of the kitchen. She has to walk past my chair to exit and it takes all of my energy to stop myself from grabbing her hand, from pulling her close to me.

"I'm sorry," I mouth to her exiting form. "I'm so very sorry."

38

RORY

Just like that, it's all over. After collecting my things, I drive my car away from Helen's in a fury. I don't know who I'm angry with. Myself most of all. For allowing myself to dream. For allowing myself to seduce her—for letting Jess spur me on like that. Because what was I thinking? That I could end up in bed with Helen, and then what? I could just walk away? It would just end there and somehow be easy?

I reach the edge of town and see the sign for Oxford. It's the last place I want to go. I feel unable to leave Upper Chewford. And there's only one place to go.

On the drive to my family's house I relive that walk into the village that fateful Sunday afternoon. If I hadn't gone on that walk, maybe none of this would have happened. *Yeah right.* Maybe if I can make myself believe that, it will be easier to get over—it will be easier to approach Professor Monohan and ask her to change her mind and be my supervisor. I can't even bear thinking about it. I might as well chuck in the whole thing. Maybe then, Helen and I will have a chance.

When I reach the driveway of my family's house, I'm ready to turn around. I have no idea what I'm doing here. Or maybe I

217

came here for a good dose of common sense. If I go to Jess, she'll put crazy ideas in my head again. She'll make me think that Helen and I can have some sort of future. If I talk to my mother, on the other hand, all hope will be immediately squashed. I can't give her any details, of course. That might induce a heart attack.

The front door swings open and George is there to greet me.

"Miss Rory, is everything all right?" The frown he's wearing wrinkles his whole face. Even George is looking his age today. Maybe I can see everything too clearly right now. Maybe that's why I know that Helen was right. She can't keep on being my supervisor. We'd just end up in each other's arms again and again, but nothing else would change.

"Yes." I give George a weak smile. "I was just in the neighbourhood and thought I'd pop in. Is Mother home?"

"I'm afraid she's not." George ushers me in. "She'll be out all day at the Relief Ships Charitable Trust fundraiser."

"Is anyone home apart from you?"

"Your father is." George takes my coat.

"Daddy's home?" I never even entertained the possibility.

"He's feeling a little under the weather."

"A little?"

"He has come down with a rather nasty bout of flu. The doctor prescribed bed rest for at least two days." George walks me into the empty drawing room. "So it's probably not wise to spend too much time with him if you don't want to catch it yourself."

I sag into a chair.

"Can I get you some tea or anything else, Miss Rory?" George asks.

I shake my head. "I'm going up to see how Daddy's doing."

"If I can't stop you." George's expression is kind.

I bound up the stairs, as though I have some excess energy I need to spend, but I knock gently on Daddy's door.

"Come." His voice sounds just as commanding as ever.

I peek my head around the door of his bedroom. He's sitting up in bed, staring at his iPad. "Rory?"

"Hi, Daddy." I head inside with a big smile on my face. At least I haven't lost the ability to smile.

"What are you doing here?"

"Seeing my ill father." I don't get too close to him. Not only because I want to keep some distance between myself and his germs, but also because it's not the Carlisle way.

He waves off my comment instantaneously. "It's just a bit of a cold. I'll be good to go again tomorrow."

"I'm sure you will." I try to sound encouraging, even though I know he doesn't need it.

"I'm afraid your mother's out all day. Some charity event. I'm not sure which one today."

I can't help but chuckle. As if I would have just popped over from Oxford unannounced to see my mother. "I was just in the neighbourhood."

His shoulders sag a little. Perhaps he's tired of keeping up the pretence of not being vulnerable to illness most of all.

"It's lovely to see you, dear." His words actually sound genuine.

"Can I get you anything? Some tea?"

"I've had five litres of tea already today, I think." He sends me a fragile smile. "What were you doing in the neighbourhood?"

I suppose I can tell him a version of the truth. "My DPhil supervisor lives in Upper Chewford."

"Really? What's his name?"

I roll my eyes. "*Her* name is Helen Swift."

He closes his eyes briefly while he nods as if to say 'of course'. I can't lay into him too much today. He's looking worse for wear by the minute. "Helen Swift... the name doesn't immediately ring a bell. Where does she live exactly?"

"One of the cottages by the river."

"Oh, near The Golden Fleece."

"Yes." Ah, The Golden Fleece. I've only been there twice in my life yet it seems to have become a significant spot for me. I probably won't be able to set foot in there for a good while. "Do you sometimes go there?"

"Once in a while." He sags against the pillows a bit more.

"I should really leave you to rest."

"No." He extends his hand to me. I stand too far away to take it. "Please, Rory, sit with me a bit. If you have the time. When do you need to see your supervisor?"

"I have oceans of time." I pull up a chair. "In fact, it might be the last time I see her," I lie.

I might not see Helen ever again, except, perhaps in passing at the university.

"Why's that?" I've never known my father to be so inquisitive about my life—not since it became clear I wouldn't be joining the family business any time soon.

"It's... we're just not a very good fit."

"I see." He falls silent and I don't elaborate. It hurts too much to even think about it. "How come?"

My gaze falls on the small stack of books on his bedside table. The top one is a Val McDermid—nothing new there. But I also recognise the name on the spine of the bottom one. H.S. Barr. One of Helen's books has made it onto my father's bedside table. She must really be on the cusp of hitting the big time then.

"Sometimes it just doesn't work out between a DPhil student and their supervisor," I say matter-of-factly. I reach for the books.

"Is it because of... the subject?" He's really not letting this one go. He must be suffering from quite the fever. Or maybe I'm not giving my father enough credit.

"No, Daddy." I glance at the H.S. Barr book I'm holding in my hands. "It's something else." I decide to change the subject. "I didn't know you liked cozy mysteries. I thought you were more of a dark thriller fan."

"George brought me that yesterday when I fell ill. Apparently it's set in Chewford. He says everyone in the village is talking about it."

I can't stifle a chuckle. "I've read it. It's good. You should give it a go."

"According to George, no one knows who wrote it. None of the bookshops know. Or, if they do, they're not telling, which only makes a bigger deal out of it, of course. You know how people are with secrets. It's pretty good marketing." He lets his gaze rest on me. "Are you well, Rory? You look a bit... off."

"It's this business with my supervisor. It's weighing on me, but I'll deal with it soon. It's just a matter of having Professor Monohan accept me." It's weird to be talking about this with my father while holding *Chewed Up in Chewford* in my hands. I never even received my signed copies. It's probably for the best, just in case I feel the need to hurl them out of my bedroom window.

"You may think I don't know you very well, Rory. But I'm your father and I do know you. Because you're like me. Which is why I won't press you for more information." He manages a smile. "I know you can't give it to me and I don't expect you to, but..." His eyes are a bit watery. "If this Helen Swift has hurt you, she'll have me to deal with."

I burst out laughing. This is not how my father speaks. It must be the flu putting words in his mouth.

He must also be serious because he keeps looking at me. "I may never have said it out loud, but I just want you to be happy."

"Daddy..." I shuffle in my seat. "Are you sure you're just suffering from the flu? It's nothing more serious that you're hiding from me, is it?" I'm genuinely worried he might have contracted a serious illness and it's making him overly nostalgic.

He shakes his head. "Doctor Perkins assured me it would all be over in a few days, but... I'm feeling a bit fragile." He sends me another frail smile—it doesn't look forced however. "But thank you for the concern. You should drop by more often."

Maybe you should get the flu more often, I think, but don't say out loud. I sit with my father a bit longer, all the while holding the H.S. Barr book in my hands, and wait until he has dozed off to make my way back down.

❧ 39 ❧

HELEN

"Helen," Sarah says after the weekly English Department meeting has ended. "I don't mean to pry, but is everything all right? You look awfully pale today." She keeps her distance from me. Maybe she doesn't want to catch whatever she thinks I'm suffering from. There's not a lot of chance of that, seeing as she's newly in love and I—I what? I'm not in love, I tell myself. That would simply be ridiculous.

"Bad night's sleep," I assure her.

"Do you want to have dinner? Have a chat?" I forget that Sarah knows me better than most.

Instinctively, I shake my head. I don't want to see her fawn all over Joan today. As happy as I am for her, I can't face any kind of lovey-dovey behaviour. "Thanks for the offer, but—"

"Who says it's an offer?" With a grin on her face, she steps right into my personal space. "I'm buying you dinner whether you like it or not."

I spot Susan, the Faculty Head, looking in our direction. I really should make an appointment with her soon. But all I want to do right now is bury myself in more work. Maybe this whole business with Rory was just a way to make me see I should focus more—and not give into distraction. I also need to discreetly check with Sarah if she's willing to supervise Rory, without giving her any details as to why. Maybe Rory and I should have come up with a cover story, but she was out the door before I had the chance to say any more. I vividly remember her ice-cold glare. How her face went from inviting to completely shut-off. I also remember—also too vividly— many of the other things that happened over the past twenty-four hours.

"Fine," I say. I don't have the wherewithal to stand up to Sarah. And I could do with a friend.

"See you in an hour at La Bottega?"

"I'll be there," I quickly say. "Please excuse me, I need to speak to Susan." I dash after Susan, who's already in the corridor, walking to her office as though she's in a great hurry. Maybe now's not the time.

No, Helen, I tell myself. Now *is* the time. I'm already out of sorts and I really shouldn't cut myself any more slack. Look where it has got me.

"Susan." Her legs are shorter than mine so I don't have much trouble catching up with her. "Can I talk to you some-time this week?"

She stops and turns to me. "Sure. What's it regarding?"

"It's... um, a personal matter." I glance around, indicating that I don't want to announce the subject in the corridor.

"Sure, give James a call tomorrow. I'm sure he can squeeze you in before the weekend." She sends me a quick smile and continues on her way.

The first step has been taken. This week I'm telling the Faculty Head that I'm H.S. Barr.

"I'm telling Susan this week." I try to keep my face as straight as possible. Telling my boss about my other activity feels so easy compared to what I'm about to say next. "And I wanted to ask *you* if..." I cast Sarah a brief glance.

"Yes?" She nods encouragingly.

"I think I made a mistake taking on another DPhil. I should have thought it through more before accepting. I can't commit to another three years. It's still early in the process. Would you consider taking over supervision of Victoria Carlisle?"

Sarah arches up her eyebrows and doesn't immediately reply. "It's not that I don't want to, Helen. But this is so unlike you." She leans back in her chair and examines my face. "When you commit, you commit." She chuckles. "I should know."

"As I said, I made a mistake." I made more than one, but I'm not going to tell Sarah about all of them. "My life has changed. *I* have changed. I feel like I need to follow through. Like this is the time to do it. I'm supervising two other candidates who should finish their dissertations this year, one of whom is going to need a lot of my time if he actually wants to graduate."

Sarah nods her understanding. "You want to focus more on your writing career?"

Her tone is so matter-of-fact, it surprises me. "Yes. I have a new book coming out soon and I'm telling Susan before the end of this week."

She slants forward. "That's great."

I narrow my eyes. "You've somewhat changed your tune."

She pulls her lips into a crooked grin. "Turns out Joan is a bit of an H.S. Barr fan."

A surge of pride swells in my chest. "Really?"

Sarah nods. "In fact, I know it would make her very happy if I brought home some signed H.S. Barr books. With a personal message to the lovely Joan written inside and all that jazz." She beams me a wide smile—as though she never criticised my books before.

And here we go again with the signed books. It takes me

right back to the conversation I had about signing books with Rory. I'm also reminded that I never signed those books for her.

"Of course. I'll bring them tomorrow." I take a sip of water. "So, will you do it? Will you take over Victoria from me?" It sounds so business-like when I say it like that, whereas inside me, this doesn't feel like business at all.

"Give me her contact details and I'll have a chat with her. We'll need to clear this with Susan as well," Sarah says.

"I'll take care of that." Could it be this easy? Is letting Rory go as simple a matter as having Sarah become her supervisor?

"You don't seem too pleased about it," Sarah says. "Something about you caught my eye in that meeting this afternoon. Something's not right with you." She drums her fingertips on the table top.

"I'm very grateful that you're willing to step in, Sarah." I try to inject some joy into my voice, but it falls flat nonetheless. "I really am. It means a lot."

"Are you worried about telling Susan?"

I'm not sure what she's referring to at first. Am I worried about telling Susan about shirking my supervisor responsibilities of Rory's DPhil? The mere thought is enough to cause more regret to course through me.

"A little." I assume, however, that Sarah's referring to my alternative career as a writer.

"If she doesn't like it, you can always quit."

My eyes grow wide—some of the things coming out of Sarah's mouth today. Next she'll confide in me that Joan's already moving in with her or something similar. Or maybe it's the effect of being in love. It has instantly mellowed her. *Love*. At least what happened between Rory and me had nothing to do with love.

"Really?" I chuckle. "Says the woman who was extremely sceptical about my writing when I first told her."

"I was just being my usual snobbish self, Helen. Would you expect anything else from me?" She refills our wine glasses, but I abstain. I'm driving home tonight.

"No. You reacted completely according to my expectations."

"Who else have you told?" she asks.

"No one." Rory's reaction springs to mind again. I suppose I should tell Sarah that she knows. It might come up if Sarah becomes her supervisor. "Well, I did tell Rory."

"You told your supervisee?" Sarah sips from her wine.

I did so much more than that, I think, but I don't say anything.

"Helen?" Sarah's voice is insistent. "Either you tell me what's going on here or I start guessing and I'm not sure that's what you want. My imagination's about to run away with me here..."

"What do you mean?"

She leans over the table and looks me straight in the eye. "At first, I thought you were so distracted because of your writing and the stress it's been causing you, but there's something else going on here. I'm not sure what, but I know *you*, Helen. Better than most, so..."

"I—" I look into Sarah's face. Her mouth reminds me a little of Rory's. Her lips are pillowy and kissable like hers. "Things have gotten so out of hand." I glance around me. Sarah managed to procure us window seats and the nearest table is far enough away as to not be able to eavesdrop on our conversation. Sarah's still slanted towards me and I meet her in the middle of the table. "Between Rory and me," I whisper.

"I knew it," she whispers back. "I just knew it was something like that. I had no idea you had the hots for your student —because that's so very unlike you, Helen—but still. I told Joan the other day. I said to her, I bet Helen's got the hots for *someone*." She pauses to take a breath. "What do you mean by things have gotten out of hand?"

I inhale deeply. "I slept with her."

Sarah brings a hand to her mouth. "No way." She narrows her eyes. "*Helen.*" She chuckles. "You slept with Rory." She reaches for her glass and takes a big gulp. "You might as well have just told me you're flying to the moon tomorrow."

"It's why I can't be her supervisor anymore."

Sarah nods. "I get it. It's unethical. So... tell me more. How long has it been going on?" She draws her lips into a crooked grin. She's enjoying this conversation a little too much.

"It happened once. Well, maybe twice. But it's over. I ended it as soon as... I could, I guess."

"Goodness me, Helen." Sarah looks like she might pat me on the back for sleeping with Rory. But then the smile fades from her lips. "That's why you're not yourself. You're upset."

"I'm angry at myself for letting it go too far. I should have stopped it much earlier. I should have asked her to change supervisor as soon as I caught a whiff of anything." The words roll quickly off my tongue. "This is not who I am, Sarah. You know that. I don't associate with students in that way."

"Do you like her?" She cocks her head. "Is that the real problem here?"

"Of course I like her," I say on a sigh, sounding very dramatic. "None of it would have happened if I didn't like her so much."

"So it wasn't just a matter of lust..." Sarah's eyes twinkle very inappropriately.

"No. Come on. Who do you take me for?"

"It's not the first time you've surprised me lately," Sarah says. "You're nothing like the Helen Swift I knew a few weeks ago. All of a sudden, you're a writer *and* you've slept with your supervisee."

"I should never have bought that bloody Porsche." I sag against the back of my chair.

"What does your car have to do with it?"

"In exactly forty-two days, I'll be fifty years old. I don't have any children. I'm not in a long-term relationship. I don't even have any pets. Clearly, I'm yearning for something I don't have and I've been acting out."

"You're being a bit hard on yourself." She rests her gaze on me. "How does Rory feel about you?"

An image of Rory's devastated features pops up in my head, followed by one of her yielding to my touch—so easily, so alluringly. "I think she quite likes me back." I take another deep breath.

"Oh, Helen. I hate to see you like this." Sarah squares her shoulders. "She shares a flat with Jess, doesn't she? They live nearby. Go to her."

"What?" I'm already shaking my head.

"I'll supervise her DPhil. You're talking to Susan this week. You might as well tell her about Rory." She holds up her hands as if to say 'voila, I've just solved all your problems'. "Go to Rory and tell her you want to be with her."

"You may think you're sitting across from a different version of me, but right now I'm having a lot of trouble recognising the Sarah Monohan I used to know." I shake my head more vehemently. "You must be out of your mind."

"What can I say, Helen? I'm in love. I'm smitten. Head-over-heels." She puts on a silly smile. "I wish everyone could feel the way I do, especially you. I care for you. I was in love with you once, Helen. Things didn't work out the way either of us hoped they would, but I'm living proof that a second chance might always be lurking around the corner."

"You falling in love with Joan is very different than me... having something with Rory. She and I are not peers. She's twenty-seven, for crying out loud."

"A good five years older than Alistair was when he met Jack. Honestly, if it hadn't been for Joan quizzing them on how they met the other night, I would simply have forgotten. And they are so happy together. What if Jack had been convinced he couldn't go through with it at the time? If he hadn't given them a chance?"

"I'm not Jack, and Rory's certainly not Alistair."

"You've said yourself that you might not want to be a professor for the rest of your working life. You have other prospects. And sometimes, when someone really special comes along, you only get so many chances."

"I'm not going over to Rory's. It's inconceivable."

"Then what will you do? Drive home in your Porsche and pout?"

"Sarah!" I have to look away from her. Sarah's the last person to be giving me a lesson in love. Besides, what happened between Rory and me had nothing to do with love. It was just a passing infatuation. Drive home and pout is exactly what I'll do. And wait until it blows over.

"I'm sorry. I know I'm coming on a bit strong." Sarah looks out of the window briefly. "Let me put it like this." She turns to me again. "If things were to go further between you and Rory—"

"They won't," I protest.

"Let me finish." Sarah's using her stern teacher voice. "You both will always be welcome at my home. I won't judge you, Helen. I've done enough of that in the past."

Sarah's words are so unexpected, they effortlessly penetrate the wall I've pulled up around me. "Thank you for saying that." While I appreciate the sentiment, it doesn't change anything for me personally.

"At least think about it. Don't just dismiss it because you deem it all so terribly improper."

"It's not an indulgence I can't allow myself."

"Looks to me, Helen," Sarah says, "you've allowed yourself the indulgence already."

She's right. I have indulged myself. Now I have to pay the price.

❧ 40 ❧

RORY

When Professor Monohan contacted me, I immediately had an inkling of what it would be about. At first, a tiny but hopeful part of me believed it would be unrelated—that Helen would have changed her mind, and wanted to continue being my supervisor. That soon proved to be wishful thinking.

I'm waiting outside Professor Monohan's office and while I appreciate her agreeing to take over from Helen, it nevertheless fills me with dread. It's a dread I can't really explain because I know it's for the best. I know Helen can't be my supervisor anymore. It would be too hard for both of us. But it also leaves me with no excuses to contact her. The best I can hope for is to run into her on campus. I spotted her the other day, hurrying towards the car park—as though rushing towards a new lover.

Helen's office is just down the hall. She could walk past at any moment, I guess. The prospect could be exciting, yet it only deflates me.

It's over and we both know it.

Professor Monohan opens the door for me and I focus on her instead of wallowing in self-pity. Everything about her is so different than Helen. She has dark hair and her eyes are light-brown—they make me miss Helen's mysterious blue gaze acutely. In a way, it also stings that they were a couple once.

"Rory. Let's sit." Sarah's way is much more informal. She leads me to a suite of sofas by the window. Helen always had me sit at her desk. "Let's talk."

"Thanks for seeing me." Maybe this won't be too bad. There's much less tension in the air in this office. I feel like I can breathe more here. Maybe I should have pushed a bit more for Professor Monohan to take me on from the start, instead of taking no for an answer so easily—then I wouldn't be in this mess right now.

"Of course." She sits and slings one leg over the other. Then she looks at me and taps a finger against her chin. "We'll get to your research in a bit." A small smile plays on her lips. "I've talked to Helen..."

The mention of Helen's name makes my palms clammy.

"I suppose she'd want me to refer to her as Professor Swift in the company of a student, but in your case..." She tilts her head. "I hardly think that's necessary."

Oh my god. She knows. Helen must have told her the real reason why she can't be my supervisor anymore. I find that very hard to believe, but I'm still pretty sure that's what Sarah's referring to.

"I believe you and Helen were quite close," she says.

I'm not sure what I'm allowed to say. I shuffle in my seat uncomfortably.

"I won't be coy with you, Rory. That's not how I want to start this relationship. I know about you and Helen."

I swallow hard. "Okay." I take a few seconds to process this information. What does it mean that Helen told her? Does it mean anything at all?

"How are you feeling?" Sarah's question sounds very sincere.

Yet I'm not certain she's someone I want to divulge my feelings to.

"I—I'm not sure—" I begin.

"I can see why the two of you might have liked each other," she says.

I fell in love with Helen, I nearly blurt out, but I stop myself. "I'm sorry, Professor Mono—"

She holds up her hands. "Call me Sarah, please."

"Sarah... this is all a bit surreal at the moment." I'm beginning to regroup.

"I know." She nods. "I was very surprised to find out how much Helen confided in you. You probably know more about her than most people—even the ones who've known her for years. The whole H.S. Barr thing for starters..." She tilts her head again. "I take it you've read the books?"

"I have."

"You're hardly an impartial judge." She paints on a smile.

"I very much am." I manage to make my voice sound utterly convincing. "I read *Chewed Up in Chewford* before I knew she wrote it and I truly enjoyed it."

"Okay." From her tone, I deduce Sarah doesn't feel the same way about it. "My partner has become quite the fan. She's read all three of Helen's books."

"Professor Fleming sent it to me after I told him that my family live in Upper Chewford."

"Ah yes, Alistair is always one to stir the pot." She draws her lips into a smile again. "He's rather good at that." Her eyes narrow. "Tell me, Rory, now that Helen's no longer your supervisor, do you have any further plans to woo her?"

The way she says it makes me burst into a chuckle. It sounds more like a joke than a question. She looks at me as though she's expecting a serious answer, however.

"Of course not." I shake my head for effect. "Helen's made it very clear that's not what she wants."

"Helen doesn't know what's good for her sometimes."

"What are you implying?" I square my shoulders.

She holds up her hands, playing innocent. "I'm not implying anything, but... I know she's rather fond of you. Much more than she would care to admit to anyone, least of all herself. That's my intel. Consider it a welcome gift from your brand new supervisor."

My heart surges. Helen has confided in her friend about me —and she must have somehow given away her feelings for me. Can I still do something about this? Is it even my place?

"I really appreciate that, Sarah."

"We should probably stop talking about Helen behind her back now," she says. She holds up a finger. "Just promise me this, no matter what happens next, treat her with respect. I didn't always do that when we were together and I know I hurt her because of it."

I nod eagerly. I'm ready to treat Helen with all the respect she deserves—if only she'll let me. Hope swells in my chest.

"Now tell me about you, Rory. Start with your family." That smile again. "Enquiring minds want to know."

They always do, I think, but I don't mind telling Sarah every last thing she wants to know. In the space of ten minutes, she has changed my entire outlook on all things Helen Swift.

❧ 41 ❧

HELEN

I sit in my car but I can't seem to find the resolve to start the engine. I don't want to leave Oxford—something about it seems too final.

I could always stay the night, but, by now I have about twenty thousand words of dictation to catch up on. Detective Inspector Orla Parish's adventures have been grossly neglected of late.

Tomorrow's meeting with Susan is on my mind but—who am I kidding?—what's really been occupying me is what Sarah said to me over dinner at La Bottega.

"You both will always be welcome at my home. I won't judge you."

She judged my hobby much harsher than she did my dalliance with Rory. But Sarah's not the same woman I was in a relationship with. She has evolved. She has Joan now. I have my writing.

I *had* Rory.

That Alistair would encourage me was hardly a surprise, but that Sarah would very much is. If she can see some sort of future for me and Rory, why can't I? And times have changed since Alistair and Jack fell in love. Besides, they're one of the happiest couples I know.

I drum my fingers against the steering wheel. Again, I feel like I have a choice to make. Wherever I drive my car next will be significant. I'm the one in charge of the car. It's my choice to make.

I start the engine and exit the car park. The drive to my chosen destination is only a few minutes.

I don't see Rory's car parked in front of her building. Maybe she has a garage somewhere. Or she couldn't find a spot in the street. Or maybe she's not home. If I ring the bell, maybe Jessica will be the one who opens the door for me. The thought of that is almost enough to make me drive away. As though Rory's roommate symbolises everything I find wrong about what's happened between us.

I feel very self-conscious sitting in my car in Rory's street. There are too many students about. I can't stay here. I have to do something—quickly.

I take a deep breath and just as I'm about to get out of the car, a knock on the window startles the living daylights out of me.

When I recognise Rory's face, both excitement and indecision wash over me again. It's the ambivalence of it all that's doing my head in the most. I need to make a decision before I drive myself completely crazy. But I think I made my decision when I drove away from the university car park.

I lower the car window. Rory's smile is much more confident than I had expected after I asked her to switch supervisors.

"Are you lost, Ma'am?" she says. "We don't get many Porsches in this street."

"I seem to be." I decide to play along while the ambivalence in my heart quickly dissipates. "Could you possibly get in and show me the way?" I mean it in more ways than one.

"My mother always taught me not to get into a car with strangers. Especially Porsches." Rory's smile grows wider.

"Really? She singled out Porsches?" I try to keep a straight face.

"Mother's very wary of Porsches. What can I say?" She opens the car door. To my relief, she gets in. "Luckily, I've never been one to heed my mother's advice."

"Lucky for me, indeed." I keep my hands on the steering wheel. I need to hold on to something. "Do you have a minute, Rory?"

"I have much more than a minute for you." Rory turns to me fully.

"Can I drive us away from here?"

"Please." Rory swivels away from me briefly to reach for her seat belt. "Take me wherever you want."

Before I start the car, I look her in the eye. "Do you want to come home with me?"

"Yes." Rory's absolute faith in me—even though I haven't even told her why I'm here—shocks me into action. And into wanting her all over again.

"You don't need anything from your apartment?"

"Hell, no," she whispers. "Just drive."

I start the car and, in silence, manoeuvre us out of the street.

I've got so used to being alone in my car it feels strange to have Rory beside me. To hear her breath. To feel her gaze on me as I negotiate the busy Oxford streets until I reach the road to the Cotswolds.

"You're not going to kick me out as soon as we arrive, are you?" she asks.

"No. I can't promise you a lot of things, but I can promise you that." I'm glad I have the road to focus on. I need to suppress my urge to kiss her. We need to talk.

"Good, because I really don't feel like calling George and

having to spend the night at my family's house." I can feel her gaze fully on me now. "Just so you know."

"Did you, um, talk to Sarah about your research?" It's not really the question I want to ask her, but I need to build up to it.

"Yes and no." Rory's voice sounds very light. I shoot her a quick glance. It's almost enough to drive me to distraction. I'd very much prefer to get us to my house in one piece. "She has agreed to supervise me, but our main topic of conversation wasn't my research. It was you."

"Me?" I feign surprise.

Rory chuckles. "It was a bit unexpected. Nearly as surprising as your car turning up in my street."

"I can't seem to stay away." Maybe it's because I'm driving, but I have no idea where that came from.

"I'm starting to notice." I hear Rory shift in her seat. I'm afraid to glance at her—afraid the grin on her lips might make it entirely unsafe for me to drive.

"I'm sorry for being so cold with you last Tuesday. I don't really know how to do this." I do glance at her now. There's no sign of a grin on her lips.

"I don't know either, Helen, but how about we try to figure it out together?" When she turns to me, she extends her arm and puts her hand on my knee. Instantly, a high-volt current of lust surges through me.

"I'm talking to the Faculty Head tomorrow."

"About us?" Rory squeezes my knee.

"About my work as H.S. Barr but I figured I should probably tell her about us while I have her attention."

"Don't tell the Head about us, Helen. Not yet. It's none of her business." Her grip on my knee softens. "It will only put more pressure on you. Just tell her about your books." She does send me a grin now. I can only enjoy it for a fraction of a second. "But I'm really proud of you for taking the step of talking to her."

It's such a strange sensation to have Rory tell me she's proud of me. I don't have students telling me such things. But Rory's much more than a student—and I'm no longer her supervisor. Maybe I can help her with her DPhil in other ways.

"Thank you," I say softly.

"Christ, Helen. Why is Chewford so bloody far from Oxford?" Her grasp on my knee intensifies again.

Her impatience brings a smile to my face. "Ah, millennials. So impatient."

"You've made me wait for you long enough already, wouldn't you agree?" she says.

I think her fingertips may leave a permanent imprint in the flesh around my knee.

❧ 42 ❧

RORY

Helen came for me. Just as I was trying to come up with the best scenario to approach her again—after my conversation with my new supervisor—I spotted her car in my street. I would recognise her, frankly, rather obnoxious Porsche anywhere.

Now, I can't wait to arrive in Chewford. It's a pain in the arse that she lives so far away, but it does give me time to think —to process. Helen strikes me as someone who wants to know all the answers to all the questions before she embarks on any adventure. And whatever is going to happen between us will be an adventure. But we don't have any answers. We have no idea what will happen next. All we know—all I know—is that I want to be with her. That when we arrive at her house and close the door behind us, I will happily stay there until we need to go out for sustenance. That's what I want. I can't be certain of what Helen wants exactly, but she came for me and that's something.

"I spoke to my father," I say, when we're only ten miles away from Upper Chewford. "After I left your house on Tuesday, I went home and he was there. He was in bed with the flu." I texted Daddy yesterday to ask how he was doing and he was back at work already, going full steam ahead as usual. "He basically told me that he just wants me to be happy."

"Did you... tell him about us?"

"Not in so many words, but, yes, I guess I did tell him. I think he understood." I rub my thumb over Helen's knee. "He said he'd come after you if you hurt me again."

"Lord Carlisle has got it in for me?" There's amusement in Helen's voice. "I'd better be on my best behaviour then." She throws in a smile. "Do you want me to make a stop at his lordship's manor? Ask his permission for what's about to happen next?"

Helen alluding to what's about to happen is enough to constrict my throat. I give a terse shake of my head.

A few minutes later, she parks in front of her house. I do hope her nosey neighbour isn't home, and if she is, that she leaves us in peace. I just want to get inside. I feel as though once we get behind her closed door, our chances of making it will multiply. It's not a rational thought but none of this is very rational. We're just two people who can't keep away from each other. It's the oldest tale in the history of mankind. With a few complications thrown in.

After Helen has cut the engine, she takes a deep breath. "I'm glad we're here."

"Me too." With that, we hurry out of the car and, without being accosted by Stacey, make it inside.

She leads me into the lounge. Her house is much tidier than when I was here before. Maybe agonising about what to do has put her in a clearing up mood. I wait for her to speak. She brought me here. She came for me. She has to speak first. I think my intentions are clear enough by now.

"I haven't prepared a speech," she says. She runs a hand through her hair. "We should talk, I know that much, but I don't really know where to start."

"Just tell me one thing." My intentions might be clear, and

hers might be becoming clearer, but I still need to hear it spoken out loud. "What made you change your mind?" I lean against the sofa, trying to look casual while my heart beats wildly in my throat.

"You." She fidgets with her fingers. "I can't seem to get you out of my head."

"You only asked me to change supervisor two days ago. You didn't really give it much chance." Who's the impatient millennial now?

"Maybe..." She takes a step towards me. "I didn't want to give it much chance. Maybe, I didn't really want to forget about you."

"You're supposed to be the smart one." I meet her halfway. My legs tremble as I approach.

"I might be book smart"—she pulls her lips into the beginning of a smile—"but I'm not smart the way you are." She grabs my hands. "Emotionally smart."

"No more kicking me out of your house, please."

She shakes her head. She's so close I can feel her breath rush over the skin of my cheek.

"No more badmouthing me to Lord and Lady Carlisle," she says.

"I can't wait to introduce you to them." I can already imagine the fit Mother's going to throw.

"Let's not get too ahead of ourselves." Helen pulls me closer.

"I will expect that win-me-back speech in the morning." My lips touch hers.

"It seems to me that I've already won you back."

"It never hurts to go the extra mile." I lean into her.

Helen doesn't reply with words anymore. She lets go of my hands and curls her arms around me, holding me close. She still doesn't kiss me. What is she waiting for?

I look into her eyes and I know what she's doing. She's savouring the moment. She's taking her time to commit it to memory. This might very well be the defining moment of our time together. We can't know it yet, but if it is, she'll want to be able to recall its significance.

"You've led me so terribly astray," she whispers.

"It's been the greatest pleasure of my life so far." I send her one last smile before pressing my lips against hers. Her mouth opens instantly, as if my tongue were a long-expected guest.

When we kiss—again, in her living room—I know that this kiss is different. All her intention is behind it. She may have doubts—and so do I—but right now, they're squashed by what we want. And, as if by magic, we want the exact same thing.

I want to kiss her like this until dawn and then, I want to do it all over again. In between, I also want to take a breath and look at her. Really look at her. Take her in. Remind myself that this is really happening. That even though it might be hard for us to be together, there's really no choice.

❦ 43 ❦

HELEN

"I wish I could call in sick," I hear myself saying. I want to check whether those words came from my own mouth.

"Just do it." Rory's lying on her belly in my bed, her chin propped onto an upturned palm. "When was the last time you called in sick?"

"I don't get sick very often." My lips are already drawing into a smile.

"I bet you believe that you don't have time to get ill, just like my father."

"I thought he was laid up with the flu earlier this week?"

"Exactly. Even those who believe sickness is some sort of weakness are not exempt from getting it." She scoots a little closer to me.

"But I'm not ill." I run a finger through Rory's hair. "The only thing I seem to be suffering from is a bout of insanity."

"I would call it acute sexual desire." Rory shifts her weight and puts her hand on my belly. "I'm sure that's an acceptable reason to not turn up for your lectures today."

I snicker. "I have my meeting with Susan, the Faculty Head, today. I'm coming out of the closet."

Rory's hand stays mercifully still. "Will you request to reduce your hours next term?"

"That's the plan." I find her hand under the sheets and run a finger over her knuckles. "Because yet another distraction has been added to my life."

"Am I keeping you from writing?" Rory slants her head.

She is, of course, but I don't want to give Rory the impression she isn't more than welcome here—I've done enough of that. "I'll make up for it later."

"Do you want me to catch the bus back to Oxford so you can dictate in the car?" Her hand travels downward.

"I will not be the one responsible for having Victoria Carlisle use public transport." I chuckle.

"You're so very considerate, Helen."

I turn on my side and press myself against her naked body. "Will you come and stay with me this weekend? You can work and I can do some writing."

"Depends." She gazes into my eyes. "Have you been to the shop or is it your intention to starve me again?"

I burst into another chuckle. "The fridge is fully stocked, milady."

"Then my answer to your question is a thousand times yes."

"Good." I pull her close.

"Will you then finally give me those signed books I asked for weeks ago?" Rory whispers in my ear.

"That and so much more," I whisper back.

We lose ourselves in a kiss again and I wish I could stay in bed with Rory all day long. But I don't want to postpone my appointment with Susan. I need to tell her. Afterwards, I can celebrate with Rory by my side all weekend long.

I'm not as nervous as I thought I would be. Maybe it's the

effect of waking up next to Rory. Now that I've given myself full permission to be with her, that's one weight lifted from my shoulders.

I will have to tell Susan about Rory at some point. But today's not that day.

"She's waiting for you," Susan's assistant says as I arrive.

I knock on the door and realise, now that I've told Alistair and Sarah—and Rory—this isn't such a big deal anymore.

"Helen, please be seated." I've known Susan Wainwright for as long as I've been at Oxford. We were colleagues first, until she became the boss. I remember what Sarah told me about being next in line for Faculty Head. I have considered the option on various occasions in the past—before H.S. Barr was born.

Susan leads me to a pair of club chairs by the window. She does have a lovely office.

"Tea? Coffee?" She winks at me. "Something stronger? It's Friday afternoon, after all."

"I'm fine, Susan." I sit down and think about how I could never leave this place completely. I was a student here. I lived in town for almost twenty years—until I bought my cottage in Upper Chewford. So many of my memories are tied up here in Oxford. "But please feel free to partake." I send her a big smile.

She waves off my comment and sits down across from me. "I hear you're no longer supervising Victoria Carlisle," she says. Hearing Rory's name knocks me off balance for an instant.

"That's right. Sarah's taken over."

"Care to tell me what the problem was?" She rests her gaze on me.

Maybe she's under the impression that this is what I wanted to talk to her about in this meeting. I do owe her an explanation. "Both Ro—Victoria and I believed Sarah would be a better fit for what she's trying to accomplish. That's all."

"If everybody's happy about the outcome." She doesn't seem

intent on digging deeper into this. "That's what's most important."

I nod.

"How many DPhil students do you have under your supervision now?"

"Two fourth-years and one third-year," I say. "It's iffy whether both the fourth-years will graduate this year, however."

"It's still early. You can get them there, Helen."

I think the time for small talk has passed. "I will. I'll make it a point of pride to do so." I pause. "I wanted to talk to you about something else. Something that might catch you off guard a bit."

"Shoot." Susan looks as though nothing much has caught her off guard in the past decade—since she became Faculty Head.

"Three years ago, I started writing fiction." I must thank Alistair and Sarah for, unwittingly, preparing me for this moment. I'm no longer nervous about telling someone I'm also H.S. Barr. I'm proud. "Cozy mysteries set in the Cotswolds. The books have somewhat taken off and it's been occupying more and more of my time."

Susan just nods. She doesn't seem surprised at all.

"I effectively find myself working two full-time jobs since the term has started and... it's been a bit much. Moreover, I'll be fifty—"

"Helen," Susan stops me. "I really enjoyed *Chewed Up in Chewford*."

"W—what?" I haven't given her any titles yet.

"I know you are H.S. Barr, writer of mysteries set in the Cotswolds and the greater Oxfordshire area."

My jaw slacks and it takes a few seconds before I get my bearings again. "How do you know?"

"It's my business to know." Her eyes sparkle.

"That might be so, but I always believed I kept my writing identity hidden very well."

Susan smiles warmly. "I received an email a few weeks ago from one Andi Morris, claiming a member of my faculty was the writer H.S. Barr. I didn't pay any attention to it at first, but it somehow kept nagging at me. Once I looked up H.S. Barr and found out the title of the first book, the penny started dropping."

"Andi Morris?" I never even replied to her. I make a mental note to do so as soon as possible—and give her a piece of my mind. Or actually, come to think of it, she's not deserving of my reply after the stunt she pulled. "How dare she contact you?"

"I agree. It's not her place to tell me." Susan sits up a little straighter. "But I'm glad *you* are telling me now, Helen."

"You read *Chewed Up in Chewford?*" I need to make sure I heard that correctly.

"I did. I do like a good cozy." Susan sounds genuine. "I'll be reading the next one soon."

"I'll bring you a copy next week." I sit there beaming.

"That would be lovely. Will you sign it for me?" Again with the signing. If even Susan prefers a signed copy, my reluctance about signing books must be a personal flaw then.

"Sure," I say, as though I fill my precious free time with nothing other than signing copies of my books. "This doesn't pose a problem for my position at the Faculty?"

"Seeing as you've kept the two completely separate so far, I don't immediately see why it would. Unless you tell me otherwise."

"Thank you, Susan. I really appreciate your kind reaction."

"What other reaction is there? I run the English Literature Faculty. Aside to teaching it, you are now actively *creating* English literature. If anything, it should open up new teaching opportunities." Susan isn't nearly as snobbish as Sarah, it turns out—I don't think many people are.

"About my teaching." The hardest part of this conversation is yet to come. "Would there be an option for me to no longer work full-time as of next term?"

"Ah." Susan nods slowly. "Now we come to the crux of it."

I mirror her nod.

"This isn't a prison." She draws her lips into a small smile. "Your books are selling well then, I gather?"

"I really can't complain."

"In that case, who am I to stop you?" She stands up and extends her hand. Once again, I'm reminded that my biggest fear about this existed only in my head. Maybe it's like that in other areas of life as well. Now that I've taken the leap with Rory, I hope I'll continue to have experiences like this where people react in such a lovely manner to the choices I've made.

"You don't know how happy I am to hear you say that." Instead of shaking Susan's hand, I pull her into a warm hug.

❧ 44 ❧

RORY

"Is this a dream?" I ask Helen as soon as she wakes up.

"Not sure. Am I still asleep or did you just wake me up —again?" Her lips curve into a smile.

"Excuse me, but you're doing a pretty good job of keeping me awake as well. And, statistically, I need more sleep than you." Helen when she wakes up is a true sight to behold. All her fences are down and there's nothing rigid about her.

"I'm not in the business of statistics, so." She rolls onto her back.

I scoot up to her, leaning on my elbows. "Do you want to go back to sleep? It's Saturday, after all."

She briefly closes her eyes. When she opens them again, I can see the tension in her face. "This *is* sleeping in for me. Usually, I'd be up at the crack of dawn." She brings her hands to her head.

I put a hand on her belly. "Deep breaths," I say, my tone not entirely serious. "Come next term, you'll only be a half-time professor at Oxford University."

"Hallelujah." She looks me in the eye. "While that is

wonderful and I'm so happy to have taken the leap, this seems to bring about a whole new kind of pressure."

"Helen." I make sure I do sound very serious now. "Not everything needs to be done today."

"You're right." She runs a finger over my cheek. "I think today I'll just focus on you."

"I won't be this distracting all the time." I bat my lashes. "Or at least I'll try not to be."

"If my H.S. Barr career doesn't work out, we can always move to your family's house in Scotland," I joke.

"Or you can sell this place and move into my parents' house. You can be a kept woman. Just know that it will come at a price."

"What's the price?" Her finger's already travelling down. She was all over me all night long, but neither of us can get enough of each other.

"Mother's judgment and, well, my father already has it in for you, so..."

"At least there's the butler." Helen smiles at me.

"Good old George, yes. Although I think he must be close to retirement age."

"I'd best make a go of the writing then."

"It's advisable." I pause to glance at her. At her delicious lips that have given me so much pleasure already. "As long as you make a go of us as well."

"I believe that's what I'm doing right now." Her fingers have reached the apex between my thighs.

"Wait..." I bring my face as close to Helen's as possible without touching her. "Who am I waking up with this morning? Professor Swift or H.S. Barr?"

"Who do you want to wake up with?"

I look her in the eye. "Professor Swift, my former DPhil advisor who led me astray, of course."

"I did not—" Helen starts to protest, but I cut her off by kissing her on the lips.

"Are you sure?" I ask. I already have my hand on the door knob.

"It's just a stroll," Helen says, "unless you have plans to kiss me in the middle of the village green."

"Should I walk behind you at a respectable distance?" I open the door.

"Rory." Helen folds her arms around my waist. "I feel a thousand percent more free than I've ever done. And what's the worst that can happen?"

"We could run into Mother." I press my backside against her.

"If you ever have any intention of introducing me to your mother, you should perhaps highlight some other, more positive attributes of her personality."

"I'll try to think of some." I turn around in Helen's embrace. "Thanks for stepping out with me."

"We need some air. We've been cooped up in this house for far too long."

"Come on then." I pull myself away from her and head out. "The coast looks clear." I eye the nosy neighbour's house.

"I'm sure Stacey will be ready to greet us when we get back." We walk towards the pub together.

"How will you introduce me to her?"

"As Rory Carlisle," Helen says matter-of-factly.

I walk alongside her, my hand casually bumping against hers. She takes it and we walk into the village hand-in-hand.

"It's as though telling the Faculty Head about H.S. Barr has set you free in so many ways."

"It has." Helen holds on to my hand a little tighter. "Because as I sat there telling her, it hit me that most of the agony over keeping it a secret could have been avoided. It was all in my head. As I walked out of Susan's office, feeling better about myself than I have in ages, I promised myself I wouldn't let it happen again. I wouldn't let myself get so caught up in useless fear like that."

"So that's what this walk is about? No longer being afraid of who you really are?" I was expecting a casual stroll through Upper Chewford, but Helen seems to be dealing with some existential issues—or, rather, she seems to have dealt with them already.

"I used to give Sarah such a hard time about it when we were together. She didn't want anyone at work to know about us for the first two years we were an item. I pressured her to come out and maybe that was wrong of me, because I now know how she felt. She was afraid. And it doesn't matter that the worst of what she expected to happen was all in her head. It was there. It was real for her. I've felt that fear now. And I don't want to feel it again. I actively want to fight against it."

"Happy to be of service." I lean into her a little.

"That's the funny thing about you and millennials in general. You've been raised with so much less fear and trepidation. You have all this... unbridled confidence."

We cross a tiny bridge over the river that runs alongside Helen's house. Most of the trees still have their leaves and create a canopy of autumn colours to walk along.

"You have so much confidence about the things that my generation prefers to agonise over," Helen continues.

"You should meet Jess. She's not a Carlisle so she's a millennial without a smidgen of Carlisle guilt. Her confidence is through the roof."

"I have met Jess."

Helen stiffens slightly beside me. A middle-aged couple is heading in our direction. It's all well and good to say no to fear in theory. I think the first real practical test is coming up.

When we pass the couple, they nod. We nod politely back.

"Anyone you know?" I ask.

"No. Probably tourists." Helen doesn't let go of my hand.

We've reached the village square. "This place is truly adorable." My gaze lands on the facade of a shop called The Ultimate Scoop. "Since you've hardly fed me—again—I wouldn't mind an ice cream."

"Excuse me. I offered you a wide choice of food items but you were only interested in one thing." We stop outside the ice cream shop.

"I was only helping you get rid of your fear."

"I guess you deserve an ice cream for your efforts." Helen sends me a smile but, before we head inside the shop, lets go of my hand.

"Hi, Helen," the woman behind the counter says.

"Good afternoon, Ellie."

Just like when I was in the pub the first time, the woman behind the counter is making my gaydar ping. This one doesn't have an American accent, though. I must quiz Helen about Upper Chewford being a hotbed of lesbianism. Who would have thought?

"What can I get you?" Ellie smiles broadly at me.

"Rory?" Helen asks.

"I'm browsing the options." I smile back at Ellie. "Helen, you order first."

While I scan the ice cream flavours on offer, I wonder if I've somehow landed in an alternate universe. In the space of a few weeks, everything about my life has changed.

"Strawberry, please," Helen says.

"I'll have a cone with one scoop of chocolate chip and one of vanilla," I say.

I look at Helen while Ellie prepares our ice creams. "How's Natalie?" she asks.

"Doing very well. It's busy at the shop. Tourist season simply won't end." Ellie offers Helen her ice cream. "But you won't hear either of us complain about that."

"It never ends these days," Helen says.

It's funny to witness Helen engaged in small talk. It makes her look more human, more accessible to me. Although I already seem to have all the access I want.

"Here you go." Ellie holds my gaze while she hands me my cone. "Enjoy." I bet Ellie's gaydar is buzzing just as loudly as mine.

We say our goodbyes and exit the shop.

"Is Upper Chewford a secret lesbian enclave?" I ask before going to work on my ice cream. "The one from the pub, the American, she's a lesbian as well, isn't she?"

"Josie." Helen nods. "Yes, we do seem to have had a bit of an influx of late." She points at the next-door shop. "Ellie's girlfriend, Natalie, runs the Yolanda distillery shop."

The name of the shop rings a vague bell. "Do they sell gin?"

"Yes. And whisky."

It's the name of the gin Alistair and I got completely plastered on a few weeks ago. I wisely don't share this information with Helen. I'll tell her some other time.

"Do you want to go have a look?"

"Sure." I might as well. I think I might be spending quite some time in Upper Chewford and I should really get to know the village where I grew up, but hardly ever visited.

"We can go to the pub for dinner," Helen says. "I'll properly introduce you to Josie and her girlfriend Harry. I have some good news I want to share with them."

❧ 45 ❧

HELEN

Today, I'm fifty, and my birthday party is looking vastly different from what I had imagined it would look like. I'm launching the fourth book in my DI Orla Parish series in a physical book shop—book signing included.

My fiftieth is so different to my forty-ninth birthday, which I mainly celebrated by buying a Porsche. I had Alistair, Jack, and Sarah over for dinner—who entertained themselves by cracking jokes about my obvious midlife crisis—and that was it.

Today, I'm reading out loud from my new book, *Garrotted in Gatbury*, to a room full of people—and I think I might even enjoy it. Years of teaching have left me no stranger to lecturing to small crowds, but, of course, this is different. I'll be reading something I wrote.

It was Rory who pushed me to do this.

"Either I officially introduce you to my parents or I throw you a big book bash," she said.

In the end, it was an easy choice to make. Not that I'm afraid to meet Lord and Lady Carlisle—I actually look forward to it—but I fear they might not be so keen to make my acquaintance. The older woman who snatched up their daughter.

"Stop referring to yourself as 'the older woman'," Rory has told me over and over again. "You're turning fifty. That's all. You know what us millennials call fifty? The new thirty-five!"

So here I am, a fifty-year-old woman about to read a passage from her new book. For the last few weeks—since the new term started—I've been working part-time at the university. The prospect of that alone has given me the energy to finish this book and get on with the next one—although that renewed energy might also be due to letting someone fully into my life, without giving in to any residual fear.

Rory has become a permanent ray of sunshine in my life. When I'm with her, I'm always happy, because the opposite is impossible.

"Are you ready?" she asks. "Everyone's here."

I glance at all the chairs that, fifteen minutes ago, were empty. Now they're all full and it looks like the entire village has turned up for the event. Stacey and Marc are here, of course. Even Mireille and her girlfriend are present. Sarah, Joan, Alistair and Jack came down from Oxford, and so did Rory's best friend Jess with her boyfriend, whom, as I understand it, Rory really can't stand. She assured me she's working on it.

Josie, who I made very happy when I told her I'd have time to run the weekly pub quiz again, is here with Harry. So are the other members of Upper Chewford's 'secret lesbian enclave' as Rory likes to call it, Natalie and Ellie.

Much has changed since my last book came out. Everybody knows now. Everyone's here.

"I can't believe it," Rory says. "That man over there by the door with the very bushy eyebrows, that's George!"

"The butler?" I look at the man. His posture is as straight as a soldier's, his suit black and pristine.

"Maybe he's a fan. Come on, I'll introduce you." Rory's level of excitement was already pretty high, but it has just skyrocketed.

If I'm not going to meet the parents any time soon, I might as well meet the butler. I can't help but smile. Some parts of my life have become so extraordinary since I've let Rory into it. As we head over to George, I fully realise that, without her, I wouldn't be doing this today.

Maybe it started when we met that day in my office, although that's impossible to know. But she has been pushing me into this version of myself ever since she kissed me. A version of Helen Swift I've come to like quite a bit.

Rory introduces me to George who shakes my hand with an iron grip. Did he just give me a discreet but thorough once-over?

"I have your mother and father in the car, Rory," George says. "Your father insisted I come in first to ask you if it was okay if they joined tonight's celebrations."

"Mother and Father are here?" I can literally see Rory's jaw drop.

Just then, Harold, the bookshop owner, taps me on the shoulder.

"We should really start, Helen. It's ten past eight already."

"I'll be right there," I assure him, then put a hand on Rory's shoulder.

"If you want them to," George says.

"Of course I want them to." Rory turns to me. "No pressure, Helen."

"Meeting the parents, eh." Something surges through me but I'm not sure if it's just nerves or something else. I'm already quite nervous about doing the reading and the book signing afterwards. I suppose I can throw in meeting Rory's parents. "You must be quite serious about me."

"I'll bring them in right away." George exits the shop.

"Helen." Rory kisses me on the lips. "I've never been more serious about anything in my life."

❦ 46 ❧

RORY

"You must come to dinner, Helen," Daddy says. He sounds as though he means it. I suspect he's become a fan of H.S. Barr. He's holding his just-bought copy of *Garroted in Gatbury* as he addresses Helen.

"I would love that very much." Now that the reading's over, Helen's much more relaxed—despite this impromptu chat with my parents. As a university lecturer, she doesn't have to deal with students' parents very often. Then again, I'm not one of her students.

Mother doesn't say anything. She needs a bit more time to warm to someone and she's not the type to enjoy the kind of books H.S. Barr writes. But she's here and that means something. She could have so easily pretended to have another function to go to.

"Rory will figure something out, I'm sure," Daddy says. Arranging dinner details is not his forte. He casts his gaze to me briefly. It's hard to read him in this situation. Both my parents are nothing if not extremely polite to people they're being introduced to. They're very adept at hiding their true feelings.

"I will," I say, resisting the urge to take Helen's hand in

261

mine. I figure it would make her feel uncomfortable to hold my hand in front of my parents. I look at George who, in unguarded moments, doesn't go to the trouble of hiding his disdain for certain people or situations. But he has an actual smile on his face. When I catch his glance, he shoots me a quick wink.

"How long have you been at Oxford?" Daddy asks Helen. It makes sense for him to focus on that particular part of her life. Thank goodness she isn't a full-time writer yet.

While Helen chats to my father, I scan my mother's face. In a way, I can acknowledge this might be doubly hard for her, what with her never having fully accepted that I don't fancy men, and now coming face to face with the woman I've chosen to be with. A woman who's closer in age to her than to me. But it's about time she came to grips with the fact that life isn't always how you want it to be. I've never once apologised for my sexual preference and I'm not about to start now. What I do want, however, is a non-frosty atmosphere when Helen comes to dinner.

"Helen," someone who's been hovering around our circle for a while says. "Can I ask you a quick question before I have to dash?"

"Please excuse me," Helen says to Father.

"Of course." Daddy sends her a wide smile. He seems taken enough with her. "Don't let us keep you. This is a big night for you."

The man engages Helen in conversation and she turns away from us, leaving me alone with my parents—and their possible judgment.

"What a lovely woman." Daddy's still holding on to the book.

"Hm." That's all Mother comes up with.

I glance at Helen from the corner of my eye. My father's one hundred percent correct: what a lovely woman. I'm not about to come to Helen's defence just to persuade my mother of just how lovely she is. She can come to that conclusion herself—or she can't. It's her choice.

"You should read the book, Margaret," Daddy says. "It's really good."

"You know I don't read that kind of fiction." Mother nearly spits out the last word—as though what Helen writes hardly qualifies as fiction.

"The Carlisles! What a surprise." Jess has approached, saving my mother from whatever snobbish thing she might say next. To my surprise, it's not Jess' new boyfriend following her, but Sarah. "May I introduce you to both my and Rory's DPhil supervisor?" She points at Sarah. "This is Professor Sarah Monohan."

"Ah," Daddy says in his inimitable way, "it's just full of Oxford academics here today. I went to Lincoln College myself. So did our son. You can imagine how heartbroken I was when Rory decided to go to Cambridge instead of Oxford. Luckily, she eventually to her senses."

I have no doubt Sarah will wrap my father around her little finger in no time. I look away from their conversation just as Helen turns towards us again. She's standing right next to my mother and their gazes meet. For the first time this evening, my mother's smile seems genuine. Helen smiles back at her warmly. It's only a tiny moment of recognition, of possibility, but it fills me with such hope.

It may take time, and many a Carlisle family dinner, but Mother will learn to appreciate Helen the way she does Brenda. How can she not?

Someone else catches my mother's eye and she waves at a woman she must know from the village. I take the opportunity to stand closer to Helen.

"It's not easy to charm a Carlisle, you know," I whisper in her ear.

"Really?" she whispers back. "You could have had me fooled."

We both chuckle and I lean into her a little. "You've met my family, so it must be official now."

"It's all out in the open," Helen says on a sigh. It sounds like a contented one. "As it should be." She curls her arm around me and, in front of my mother and father, pulls me close to her.

ACKNOWLEDGMENTS

Over the years, I have collected a steady crew of collaborators who work with me on my books: my trusted editor, Cheyenne; my proofreader Claire; my forever beta-reader and friend Carrie; and my ultra-dependable better half/second-draft writer/cover designer Caroline. They all make my books so much better than I could ever make them on my own.

For this book, I enlisted two special beta-readers to shed some light on academia and getting a DPhil/PhD in particular (two areas I know next to nothing about.) Gaby and Haya helped me avoid the biggest gaffes, for which I'm very grateful. For the sake of my story, I have taken some liberties with academic procedures. Therefore, all errors are entirely my own and have nothing to do with Gaby and Haya's much-appreciated input.

I've co-written books with both Clare Lydon and T.B. Markinson. It was a privilege both times—and also such fun to work together with fellow lesbian fiction authors. The Village Romance Series was born from our desire to collaborate more, but in a different way. Writing can be solitary sometimes and it's been wonderful to have regular conversations with two smart and delightful writers.

I also need to thank you, Dear Reader, for sticking with me through my break. It has done me the world of good to take my foot off the writing gas pedal for a few months. I had so much fun writing Helen and Rory's story because it brings together a bunch of my favourite tropes (age gap—always!—being the most prominent one). I felt the pure, true joy of writing during the first draft of this book, and now writing is all I want to do again.

Thank you.

ABOUT THE AUTHOR

Harper Bliss is a best-selling lesbian romance author. Among her most-loved books are the highly dramatic French Kissing and the often thought-provoking Pink Bean series.

Harper lived in Hong Kong for 7 years, travelled the world for a bit, and has now settled in Brussels (Belgium) with her wife and photogenic cat, Dolly Purrton.

Together with her wife, she hosts a weekly podcast called Harper Bliss & Her Mrs.

Harper loves hearing from readers and you can reach her at the email address below.

www.harperbliss.com
harper@harperbliss.com

69575839R00161

Made in the USA
Middletown, DE
21 September 2019